Sophi

UNSPEAKABLE THINGS

SOPHIE KERSEY

HOLDEN
PARK
BOOKS

First published in 2018 by Holden Park Books

ISBN: 978 1 99977 692 3

Cover by Spiffing Covers

Inside pages by Carol Turl Graphic Design

Author photograph by Roddy Paine Photographic Studios

Dedication

To my dearest Jon, Ben and Sam
and to Emma, as promised.

Acknowledgements

With thanks to Lorna Fergusson at Fictionfire for her invaluable insights, Sylvia for encouragement and for blazing the trail and Jon for picking up the pieces.

CONTENTS

CHAPTER ONE

'All that fuss about the long-lost uncle,' said Deb. 'And he's a no show after all.'

Sarah surveyed the ordered beauty of the reception from the top table. Cutlery shone in the sparkle from the chandelier, reflecting her lavender theme. She shrugged against the taut silk of her wedding dress. 'I know. I've half been looking out for him all day. But you know what? I'm letting it go now.'

It hadn't been her fuss anyway. 'We don't want to hog the whole church, Sarah,' Jim's mum had kept saying. 'Isn't there anyone else you want to invite?'

There was only her brother, David, to represent the family. Dad had had a fatal stroke eight years ago. Her mother had died when she was four. People didn't usually make such an issue of it, but apparently a wedding was different.

Sarah had filled her pews with friends and colleagues – the whole editorial department had come. But her inlaws' sympathy had niggled at her. Finally she had unearthed Dad's tatty old address book from a drawer crammed with remnants of his life. Inside she had found the details for this uncle – her mother's only relative – and sent an invitation.

Well, everyone she cared about was here – leaning back in the lull after the speeches, full of goodwill and laughter, ties loosened, jackets off, high-heeled shoes dangling from toes under the tables. Her university friends were telling David that his speech was hilarious. Jim was circulating, high on all the good cheer, and she saw him now heading back to join her amid ribbing from his mates.

Deb – her bridesmaid and sister-in-law all rolled into one – touched a warm hand to hers. 'Of course. Who needs him? It's all lovely.' They had been best friends since they were eleven.

Sarah ran her fingertips over her bridal arrangement of curls. Should they move into the other room so the staff could prepare for the evening do? She had a sense of treading water, while all above the surface was serene.

'All right my darling?' Jim sat down beside her, a grin on his boyish face. A camera flashed and Sarah turned to see an array of phones raised towards them.

'Someone takes a picture whenever you come near me!'

'It's the way he looks at you,' Deb said.

Sarah leaned into Jim, feeling the muscles of his arm beneath his suit fabric. 'I'm going to the loo,' she said, under the rising hum of chatter. 'There's confetti in my knickers.'

She was heading across the soft-carpeted hallway, alone for the first time that day, when a voice said, 'Oh, here's the bride.'

One of the female staff was leading a middle-aged man with a lined face and short silvering hair. He wore a pinstripe suit like the City gents you saw in London pubs after work. A dark coat was draped over his arm. Sarah had no idea who he was, and yet they had stopped, and he was looking at her.

'Sarah?' he said. 'I'm John Briers. Your uncle.'

'Oh! I'm sorry, I didn't realise.' And now the woman had left them together – left Sarah open-mouthed and searching his face – for what? A spark of fellow feeling? A likeness?

Cool blue eyes flitted over her. 'No, I'm sorry. I'm very late. It was a work issue at the clinic. It's hard to get away when you're Director. I must have missed everything.'

'No – there's still the evening. You're very welcome.' She held a hand out – a clumsy gesture, too late to be natural, but he took it and held it.

'I was delighted to get your invitation. And surprised, after all these years. But I mustn't hold you up, you were going somewhere…'

'Oh! No, it's fine.' Where had she been going? Thoughts skittered. 'Your details were in my Dad's address book. I thought it would be nice to have you here – well, to represent my mother.'

She heard her own voice and felt like a person in a play. In the room nearby, someone was addressing the reception crowd over the clamour of conversation.

'Really? Well, that's very good of you,' her uncle said with a shake of his head. 'You bear her no grudge, then?'

There was a stillness in the plush quiet in the hallway, but then a door opened with a burst of noise.

'Sarah, they're moving us into the Clarence Room. Oh, sorry!'

Sarah turned to see Deb, a thought ruptured, unfinished. 'This is my uncle,' she said. Crisp bits of confetti had sneaked down her bodice and lodged under the lace of her knickers. They had been scratching her for hours. She caught Deb's eye and gestured towards the toilets.

'Do you want to follow me?' Deb said to her uncle. 'I'm sure we can find you a drink.'

The rest of the day was a blur of impressions, wheeling round Sarah's head. When she came out of the toilets, she made for Jim – a still point at the centre of it all; a safe place with a solid floor to stand on. Clutching her hand, he cracked jokes and chatted, at ease with everyone. They cut the cake and more photographs were taken, and then greetings rang out as guests began to arrive for the evening do.

In the early hours, they were in the lift heading for the bridal suite, cheers and good wishes still ringing in her ears.

'I met your uncle,' Jim said.

'Oh, so did I. But only for a minute.'

'He runs some mental health clinic, doesn't he, in a manor house? I told him I was getting into property development, and a bit later, he said *I have a property that might interest you.* He says it's the Gatehouse to the estate – where you lived when you were little?'

Sarah could see her blank response in the mirrored wall of the lift. Her hair had kept its piled-up style, with curls cascading down. The hairgrips were pulling at her scalp.

'Oh? You know as much as I do. If not more.'

'He says if we ever want to move out of London, we should get in touch. The house has been empty since you left.'

The lift rose to a gentle halt and Sarah's insides felt abandoned way below them. It must be the tiredness, falling now like a heavy veil. The doors slid open and two lads in hotel uniforms stood waiting, their arms full of wedding gifts.

She wouldn't see John Briers again for three years.

CHAPTER TWO

The cells of the implanted blastocyst multiply rapidly and begin to form different structures. By now the mass of cells is just visible to the naked eye.

Sarah checked her reflection in her office door. *Senior Editor for History*, the label said. She tucked a curl under a clip. Inside, her gaze swept over the neat rows of colour-coded files, and she sat down, relishing the quiet.

Carla from Admin popped her head round the door and held out a large envelope. 'Hi, Sarah! I think this is what you've been waiting for.'

Sarah pulled out a disk and a typescript. 'Yes! Three weeks and two days late. It's the latest in the Social History series: *Madness and Society*'.

'Another cheery one, then!'

'There are some comedy classics, aren't there? *Poverty. Fascism. War.* We say in Editorial that the SH in the logo stands for Shit Happens.'

'Shit Happens: Madness!' Carla's cackle receded as she went off along the corridor.

Sarah flipped open the typescript. It had better be good if she was going to keep it on schedule now. The author, Eva Leary, thought nothing of delivering late at every stage, but would want the book ready for a cherished launch date. Sarah checked that the Contents list matched the plan they had discussed, ticking off headings: *Curse or Illness?; The History of Fools; The Rise of the Asylum; The Experience of Madness.* The smaller subheadings wormed their way into her thinking: *Paranoia, Psychosis, Schizophrenia, Depression...*

She began to scan the text, dipping into tales of lost reason and ruined lives. First-person accounts snagged at her attention: *These drugs have taken away all ambition, imagination, memory and intelligence... I should have been in the prime of my life but everything was falling apart… I was more at peace after the surgery, but part of my soul was missing*. She made herself focus on an overview: the book seemed well written, but some of the ideas faltered and lost their way. Eva could be touchy about changes, but history should make sense. If the ideas didn't progress and come to conclusions, what had anyone learned? Sarah's mind began to buzz with additions and deletions, and she scribbled queries on a notepad.

When she raised her head, over an hour had passed. She reached into her briefcase to check her phone and her knuckles brushed the paper of the chemist's bag. A wave of urgency fizzed against her ribcage: she was caught in the fork between two different lives: a yes or a no. But there was no time to think about it, she had to prepare for a meeting with the editors in her team.

It was evening in the bathroom of their flat. The nerve-shattering noise of the building work had finally halted, leaving the usual London traffic hum, punctuated by horn blasts and sirens. Sarah was staring at the marbled tiles above the bath.

After three minutes, timed precisely, she let herself whirl round. On the rim of the sink was a plastic indicator. In the window was a plus sign. Sarah's gut swooped as if the floor had moved. Grasping at cold porcelain, she dropped her watch. *I must be overjoyed.*

She sat down on the edge of the bath, staring at a tremor in her leg. How many times had she imagined telling Jim that the test was positive? But she couldn't move.

A sound screamed through the flat. The smoke alarm. She heard Jim running and swearing, then pots clanging. The alarm bipped to a stop and footsteps sounded along the hall.

'You all right? The tea was burning.'

She pointed towards the plastic indicator: 'Look! Don't touch it – I weed on it!'

'Sarah!' He sat down and enveloped her in a muscular hug, his salt skin and aftershave scent coming through the tang of the train on his clothes. 'You are pleased, aren't you?'

'Yes. I just felt – funny. I mean, pregnant? How can I be?'

'What do you mean, you nutcase? We were trying, weren't we? After all that shagging, I'd be worried if you weren't.'

They went through the flat to the kitchen, still holding one another, bumping into doorways. Sarah concentrated on loosening the chicken casserole from the bottom of the pan.

'Can I call Mum and Dad?' asked Jim.

'No! Not yet. I mean, we should wait a few weeks.' Watching the casserole pouring from the ladle, she wondered if the odd feeling in her stomach was hunger or not.

Jim took an enthusiastic forkful . 'God, what are we going to be like? You and me? As parents?'

She swept a hand over the tabletop and stared at the grey film on her fingertips. Things crowded, clamouring, into her head. Lately when she came home, everything seemed coated in a layer of grime, sent in gritty wafts by the builders on either side. She saw herself singing a lullaby while pile-drivers battered the earth.

'We'll have to move,' she said, watching his face. This building was his first property success, and the flat was their prize. He had turned out to be a trail-blazer, buying the house in a run-down area and converting it into flats, but now the same thing was happening all around them. 'I know, Jim, I love this flat as much as you do, but it has got ridiculous.'

She stood up and he grasped her round the middle. 'I suppose we always said we'd move if we were having a baby.'

'Yes! And we are now. We are having a baby.' She felt a smile spring into life at the joy of it – but then there it was again, the swallow-like swoop of descent. Was vertigo a symptom of pregnancy? She reached for a notebook and pen. 'We need a To Do list.'

'One. Open beer. Two. Celebrate. Three. There isn't a three... All right. We're listing,' he said, a hand finding her shoulder and squeezing.

She got it all down, about estate agents, mortgage advisers and establishing a search radius, and he had a beer, and she didn't, in honour of the new life inside her.

But that night her mind churned over it all long after Jim was asleep. Finally she got up, fumbled through the darkness and lifted the lid of the blanket box at the foot of their bed. She'd never sleep now unless she found it.

She and her uncle had exchanged polite notes after the wedding, and then Christmas cards in the years since. Searching by the light from her phone, she found three cards and discarded two. When she opened the third one, a compliments slip fell out. Sarah almost cheered in the cold digital glare. The slip was marked 'Woodlands Clinic, Ashbury, Kent'. Underneath she saw 'John Briers' and an email address.

CHAPTER THREE

The Reception area was the smartest part of the clinic. Here, the dank sandstone of the manor house was enhanced by fittings in chrome and glass and tasteful prints on the walls. If you were an anxious relative, you might tell yourself you were leaving your loved one at a health spa in a country hotel – as the Director, John Briers, had intended. He strode away now into the dimmer depths of the building, his footsteps ringing out in the cavernous corridor. As he turned a corner, a high-pitched moaning came from somewhere nearby. He tweaked at his shirt sleeve and adjusted a cufflink.

He pushed open a door to a sparsely furnished hospital room. On the edge of the bed, an old man sat in sagging Y-fronts, rocking back and forth.

A startled nurse looked up from a loaded drugs trolley. 'Morning, Mr Briers.'

He took in her name badge along with her wide, Asiatic face and heavy breasts. 'Good morning, Patricia.'

She handed him the clipboard from the bottom of the bed, fumbling in her hurry. The dosage was a hefty one; it was surprising the old boy was awake, let alone sitting up. He watched the nurse's nervous fingers dropping a hail of pills into a plastic tub; perhaps caught slacking and trying to make up the time.

The patient rocked on and on. His expression was frozen, eyebrows raised, mouth slack, like some mocked-up impression of anguish. Briers turned to leave. If you stayed too long, you felt dragged down towards a dismal level of existence. His thoughts ran on ahead, to the end of his round and the more fulfilling visit that awaited him.

The tower patient sat in her chair by the barred window, gazing through tangled hair at the treetops below. An ancient memory shifted – of being down there in the blackness: lost, frightened, unable to get home. It disintegrated before she could grasp it.

Footsteps echoed in the well of the spiral staircase. At the scrape of his key in the door, she tried to sit up straighter. But there was always this heaviness. Sometimes she was dizzy from just lifting her head. As the door opened, chill air dried her bottom lip. It stung when she licked it, but her tongue flicked out again. His shoes made a gritty noise on the lino, coming towards her.

CHAPTER FOUR

8 weeks: The baby is still smaller than your nose, but his heart is pumping vigorously. You may not have much appetite if you are feeling sick, but a good diet is important throughout pregnancy.

'David! Can you do Joe's bath, please, I need to get the curry on,' Deb called up the stairs.

His voice came down from his attic study. 'I'm really close to finishing this module. I could do with another half-hour.'

'You said you'd do bedtime! They'll be here at eight!'

'All right! Point taken! Christ, it's only Sarah and Jim.'

'Yes but I don't want to actually poison them, so I need to get the chicken on soon.' She heard a slam and then David's clattering descent and he appeared with his hair all over the place; the picture of a distracted scientist. 'Joe, Daddy's doing bath-time! Isn't that fun?' She transferred their son's warm weight from her hip into David's awkward grasp.

'No!' he wailed. 'Not Daddy! No!'

In the kitchen, Deb made rapid preparations for browning chicken legs, trying to ignore Joe's cries from upstairs and David's questions as the fat began to spit.

'What? I can't understand you when you talk like that. Stop crying and tell Daddy clearly.' She heard Joe's crying going up a gear.

Deb had longed for this evening, especially for time with Sarah who, as well as being David's younger sister, was her dearest friend. She glanced at the kitchen pinboard with its montage of snapshots: the four of them in bars and at parties; on a beach; sitting smiling on a dry-stone wall; the colours gone lurid over time. Now that her days were filled with the mind-numbing chatter of the nursery run, it lifted her spirits to be with people who had known her before.

There was a thudding sound and Joe arrived, naked, wet and whining. He threw himself at her legs.

'So, that went well,' David muttered from the doorway.

'What's the matter?'

'He wasn't having it. He wants you. I can't understand a word he says when he's moaning.'

'Oh for–!' Deb turned off the gas cooker, snatched Joe up and tried to warm him in her arms as she stalked towards the stairs. 'All right, darling. It's all right. Let's get you in the bath again. We'll play with Sailor Man, shall we?' In the bathroom, she handed him his favourite bubble bath bottle, and he climbed into the bath with a spring in his step.

Deb heard David coming upstairs, no doubt heading for the attic. On the bathroom floor was the textbook for the next Open University module: *Pure Mathematics, Group Theory (B)*. She had been unsure about him taking time off work to study – they were hard up already with her not working. But she had imagined that in between supply teaching, he'd spend more time at home with them.

'I'll get on then, if you're OK,' he said, passing the door.

Sarah stepped across the threshold into Deb's tight hug. Her friend had answered the door wearing overstretched leggings and an old shirt of David's.

'Oh God, look at you two, all smart-casual perfect,' Deb said. 'I was going to change, but Joe wouldn't settle.' She turned her head and bellowed up the stairs: 'DAVID!'

Sarah eyed the assault course of toys in the hallway and the scientific journals in unstable piles on the stairs. Deb ushered them into the dining room and left them while she rushed to the kitchen. The table, laid for the four of them, was surrounded by teetering, pushed-back towers of mess. The mantelpiece was a jumble of photographs; the chronicle of Deb's family. Sarah found herself staring, despite knowing them by heart. She remembered going round to tea in the first year of grammar school. 'We're so glad she's got you,' Deb's mum, Janice, had said. Sarah had caught her friend's mute look of fury. 'They're getting a divorce,' she said upstairs, and burst into tears. As both her parents set up with new partners, Deb was allowed Sarah round whenever she liked. 'Just come in, love, and don't mind the mess,' Janice would say, a baby clutched to her chest; a toddler wailing up at her. The chaos was a tonic after the heavy quiet of Sarah's house, with Dad often working late and David holed up in his bedroom. The girls were allowed to roam the town, as long as they took Deb's stepsister, Hilary. Deb moaned, but they had fun with the sparky eight-year-old even if they made out to each other that she was a burden.

Deb appeared in the doorway and saw her looking. 'Ugh that dusty old mess!'

'It's not a mess, it's lovely. Like a museum of you.'

'Museum's about right! I think I'm becoming extinct. I said to myself today, *You were in charge of an entire children's ward. How is it such hard work having one healthy child?*'

There was a fluttering in Sarah's chest. 'Where's David?'

'In his ivory tower, learning about hard sums. DAVID! They're here!'

When he finally appeared, David looked vacant and bedraggled as though he had just got out of bed. He hugged Sarah and said, 'All right, mate?' to Jim in the man-of-the-people voice he used with him.

'How's the pure maths?' Sarah asked.

'Everything I hoped for. Pure, rational and clean.'

Cries of delight rang out at the candlelit dinner table when Sarah made her announcement. Deb came over to hug her and the men back-slapped and bumped glasses.

When things had settled down, Sarah told Deb, 'I'll be back at work in time to edit the next book in the Social History series.'

'What, you timed this pregnancy to fit in with your work schedules?'

'Oh, she had the whole thing worked out,' said Jim. 'A tick in her diary for every attempt. I think there might have been a spreadsheet.'

'You see, Debs!' David laughed, 'That's how it's done! Not by accident after your best friend's wedding!'

'I didn't hear you complaining!'

'I didn't know you'd forgotten your pill!'

Deb turned to Sarah. 'Well, you be rational while you can. These days I'm moved to tears by *Puff the Magic Dragon.*'

'Yeah – I thought I'd married this hard-nosed nurse,' David said. 'But once the baby comes, Jim, it's all tears and wailing and bodily fluids... And that's just Deb.'

'Um, we've got some other news,' Sarah said when they had stopped laughing. 'About Woodlands.'

'Wherelands?' Deb asked.

David busied himself with the corkscrew, his hair flopping over his face. 'Our mother's family estate'.

'Blimey, Dave,' said Jim, 'you sound like landed gentry!'

'That would explain him being so idle,' Deb said, but the earlier laughter seemed to have dispersed.

'Well, not the manor house – that's a clinic. But the Gatehouse, where we lived when we were little. I don't remember it, but David, you must.'

He was hunched over the wine, and didn't respond.

'She wants us to go and live there!' Jim said.

The corkscrew halted with its arms in the air.

'I – nothing's decided – I just thought maybe we could all go and have a look.'

David's gaze was fixed downwards, and for a moment, no one spoke. A flush swept Sarah's skin. There was a crash, followed by an unearthly howl, and she had no idea what it was – until Deb scraped back her chair. Of course – it was Joe crying, the sound distorted by the baby monitor.

'That's all we bloody need,' David said.

Joe was in his mother's arms, racked by dry, hiccupping sobs. On the kitchen pinboard behind them, Sarah saw her teenage self in a photobooth, cheek-to-cheek with Deb.

Sarah finally managed to open a childproof lid and poured sticky liquid on to a spoon. 'What do you think is wrong?'

‘He could be coming down with something, or just teething. This helps with everything. If all else fails, I drink it.’ Sarah fed the flushed boy his medicine, but half of it dribbled from his lips. He snuggled into his mother and transferred the mess to her hair.

‘Sorry, Auntie Sarah’s rubbish.’ But Joe seemed to have found what he needed in the warmth beneath his mother’s chin, and was settling into open-mouthed restfulness. ‘I don’t know, Joe, what kind of mummy will I be?’

‘Most of us try to be the opposite of our own!’

‘How does that work for me, though? I don’t even remember mine...’

‘Oh, you can do it your own way – without worrying about all that.’ Deb touched Sarah’s arm as she moved stealthily past with her sleeping burden.

But Sarah’s mind had wandered into its fretful groove, back to the uncle and the Gatehouse.

CHAPTER FIVE

'It's just – where I worked before, prescriptions for sedatives and anti-psychotics always had a time limit or a review date... They're for acute situations, aren't they? They're not meant to be long-term.'

John Briers halted, round the corner from the nurses' station in East Wing C. When the hushed conversation tailed off, he walked up to the counter and handed some notes to a nurse he didn't recognise. Her name badge said Kim Saunders. From some agency, no doubt. Did she see the displeasure beyond his professional smile?

He thought of his senior psychiatric team as he headed towards their meeting: Baker limping on to retirement, Orr-Hughes imagining no one smelt the spirits that seeped through his pores. What did they care for time limits or review dates? Under John's father's regime, there had been forced ECT, padded cells, restraining straps on the beds – yet if you had eavesdropped in these corridors then, would you have heard his methods challenged? An odd spectre of memory loomed in the dimness.

He was a small child, and had stayed home with a temperature. Father had gone to the clinic and Mary to school. John could hear his mother in the bathroom as he padded along from his bedroom to hers. He crept into her wardrobe, pulled the door shut and waited, breath trembling; one eye pressed to the crack of the door. She was always busy, or out. He just wanted a tiny strip of her to himself. He heard her in the room, and stilled his breathing. But then there was movement, heavy and brusque, and his mother's sharp gasp.

'Edward? You bastard!' He glimpsed confusion; white skin and darkness rolling over each other in his slice of vision. 'You utter bastard! I don't want you!'

'Bitch.' His father's voice struck like a whip.

'Bastard!'

'Bitch.' He heard gasps and the screech and clang of bedsprings.

His mother's voice was muffled, suffocated, moaning and crying out. With each guttural grunt from his father, a great slap stung the air.

She caught John creeping across the room when she returned from the bathroom. 'John? What now?'

'I feel funny.'

'I should think so, wandering the house when you're supposed to be ill. Get back to your bed.'

He arrived outside the conference room now, breathless and aroused, and stood in pressured discomfort, taking time to compose himself. He would look up that interfering nurse's contract as soon as this was over. See how she liked being dismissed. Then he might have to go to the tower.

CHAPTER SIX

10 weeks: The baby's brain has developed rapidly and his inner ears are complete. Your womb is the size of an orange. You may be starting to get your energy back.

It was a serpentine path through shaded woods, thick with early summer foliage. Sarah kept thinking the undergrowth might close in altogether, but Jim was driving the BMW at his usual speed. Every turn flung David and Deb about in the back seats; she could hear their seat belts rasping and catching.

'It's really off the beaten track, isn't it?' she said.

'Miles from bloody anywhere,' David said. 'There could be undiscovered tribes.' He opened a window and a crackling rush filled the car.

'This can't be right, can it, David?' Deb asked.

'How should I know?'

'Not far now!' Sarah said.

'Can we dispense with the chirpiness?' David said. 'I'm getting flashbacks to a god-awful team-building exercise with a load of awkward science teachers.'

'Hold up!' Jim cried.

They drew to a leaf-crunching halt. A little house crouched at the end of the track, its greyed sandstone shaded on every side; leaded windows reflecting only trees. In front of the garden gate was a stooped older man in tweedy trousers.

Sarah and Jim were quickly out of the car, and Deb followed, releasing a wriggling Joe from his car seat. David hauled himself out, looking as worn out as if he had walked there.

'Andrew Lovett,' said the old man, shaking hands. 'Mr Briers is away, at a conference on alternative therapies. He asked me to show you round. My firm takes care of the maintenance of listed buildings like the Manor and the Gatehouse. I also run the local history society.'

'That must be fascinating!' Sarah said. It hadn't occurred to her that Uncle John would not be there himself.

Their guide pushed open a gate, and she had her first proper look at the house. The porch echoed the angle of an elaborate gable, pointing at the half-canopy of trees. An oversized chimney stack looked borrowed from a much larger building. Gothic arches topped the latticed windows, and forest-dark ivy crawled over the stone.

'It's beautiful!' she said. Beside her, David was rummaging in his pocket. In the time it took him to fish out his cigarettes, Joe made a lightning dash for the house. David took two strides forwards, and grabbed him by the arm.

'Joe, no! Go to mummy!' His shout silenced everyone, apart from a crow cawing overhead. David steered the shocked boy in Deb's direction. Sarah tried to catch his eye, but now he was lighting his cigarette, his gaze fixed on the ground.

'I'm afraid it all needs a thorough clean,' Andrew Lovett said, leading them upstairs. 'It has been completely shut up.' Sure enough, after the fairy-tale impression of the outside, there was yellowed, peeling wallpaper in the stairwell and a brown stain on the ceiling from some ancient leak. Sarah ran a hand ran over the chipped banister paint. It came away dirty. Her feet were leaving prints on a greyed-over carpet.

'I'm not sure how much you already know…'

'Almost nothing,' Sarah said. 'I was only four when we left. And David was six, weren't you?' The question hung in the thick air, unanswered. They reached the landing and turned into a narrow upstairs corridor that the daylight barely reached.

At the far end, Lovett swung open a door. 'The nursery,' he said.

The room had a barred window and faded brown wallpaper with stylised flowers in purple, orange, pink and turquoise. The carpet was musty-orange and felt thin under Sarah's sandals as though the underlay had perished. She turned slowly, gazing. What would the room have looked like when everything was new, with curtains hanging at the windows?

'It's so seventies!' Deb laughed.

'The decade that style forgot,' said Jim.

The room was empty except for a large cupboard, its front decorated in long-faded paint to look like a house.

'The nursery cupboard was painted like the facade of the manor house.' Lovett was breathless from the stairs, and paused between phrases. 'Edward Briers, the father of the current owner, became a psychiatrist after the war, and turned Woodlands into an asylum, as it was called then. He moved his family to live here at the Gatehouse. Perhaps they missed the big house, and the cupboard was made to remind them of it.'

Joe ran to get in the cupboard.

'Careful! It's very old!' Deb rushed after him, while Jim strolled over to the barred window. Sarah glimpsed a walled garden that conjured up stories she had loved as a child.

'When Edward died,' Lovett continued, 'everything passed to his son, John, who I understand is your uncle.'

Sarah nodded. 'Our mother was his sister, Mary.' It was like watching someone on television finding out about their ancestry. She should have brought a notebook to write it all down. Did David know any of this? He was lingering by the entrance, looking at the floor.

'Ah. Well, John took over the clinic, and after she married, Mary lived here at the Gatehouse. But there has been no one here since she passed away. Quite some years ago.' Lovett turned quickly towards the door. 'Well, as you know.'

'Boo!' Joe burst out of the cupboard with a clatter. They all feigned heart-stopping surprise, and he laughed himself into a fit of hiccups.

'You are so going to get tickled for that!' Jim said, making quick nips at his ribs, and they followed Lovett out of the room, passing a motionless David in the doorway.

'So, was this your room, you two?' Deb asked.

Sarah looked around. The room evoked no more than the vague feeling of history you get from any old building. 'Was it, David?' He shrugged and moved off after the others. The stale air in the room was left swirling, disturbed.

When Sarah caught up with the group, they were standing at the foot of a short, bare staircase leading up to a wooden door. Lovett was fiddling with keys. Jim's arm enveloped her shoulders. She could see him assessing their surroundings with the restless enthusiasm he sometimes got about properties.

'Interesting place. I wonder why your Dad moved you away?'

'I don't know. He didn't say.' Dad had not talked about any of it. She didn't even remember looking at old photographs with him, and wondered now why they had never pestered him about their dead mother, their abandoned first home. But during his life it had seemed unthinkable. Did they hesitate to test that resolute strength of his, in case it crumpled?

Lovett was trying the last of the keys. It seemed to jerk a fraction of a turn, and he gave a hopeful push with one shoulder. The door stood firm – the old man's bones might give way before it did. 'The attic,' he wheezed. 'Mr Briers must have the key. Family things stored there, I suppose.' Downstairs, Jim helped him with the stuck bolts at the top and bottom of the French windows, sending a speckling of paint on to the carpet. With a shove, the doors juddered and parted, panes rattling, and they all stepped outside.

What must once have been lawn was now a wildflower meadow, hip-high with riotous summer growth. Brambles, ferns and ivy reached over the brick walls from the woods. Sarah's hand brushed the tops of rose bay willowherb with the afternoon sunlight caught in their fluff. Had she once walked barefoot on mown grass; had she and her mother opened that gate in the wall and gone out into the woods?

'It would make a lovely home for a family. Wouldn't it?'

'Yeah?' Jim glanced at her, then back at the house. 'It has got potential. But it needs a hell of a lot doing to it. And we'd have to work out where we stand with this uncle of yours.'

She was picturing the kitchen with a scrub-top table in it, and saw herself choosing curtains and cushions; a cot for the nursery. Soft lawn underfoot; a little hand in hers. She caught sight of David's shutters-down expression.

'Look, you two have got as much right to live here as we have, David. If you think you might want to …'

'We don't.' She saw Deb start at David's snapped retort.

'But... you would say, wouldn't you? Either of you – if you've even thought about it?'

David had his head down, as Joe played a game of winding round and round his legs, singing a tuneless song.

Deb seemed to rally. 'Oh no, we're fine where we are. I couldn't face moving again – I still haven't unpacked all the boxes from last time. You really fancy it, do you?'

'Well there's a lot to sort out, but – I do like it.' She reached for the level-headed reasons. 'I really want to find somewhere before I get huge. And so far, everything we've liked has been snapped up before we've even looked at it. This is good for commuting and for local amenities. And it's much nearer you, which would be lovely – especially when the baby comes.'

'It would be great to have you nearer! Wouldn't it, David?'

Joe barged between his father's legs. Unbalanced, David made an ungainly lunge and only just stopped himself from falling. 'For God's sake, Joe!'

Joe ran to Deb with his bottom lip sticking out. They all stared as David took a fierce draw on his cigarette. 'What? Oh look, it's a bit bloody remote, isn't it, Sarah? Stuck out here in the middle of nowhere. I mean, what will you do when Jim's away?'

Was that his problem – had her pregnancy made him protective? She couldn't help smiling. 'I'll lock the door! Honestly, David, I'll be fine.' She touched a fist to his arm. 'Survivors – remember?' Years ago, she had heard a new nanny on the phone, saying, 'Poor, motherless things.' She had worked out that she was talking about her and David. 'Well, she is wrong,' Dad had said, plonking his glasses down on the desk in his study, where they had gone to find him. 'You're not poor motherless things. You're survivors.' He had put the glasses back on and nodded, releasing them to return to their play.

'Don't you think it would be a lovely place for a child?' Sarah said to Deb. 'In the country, but only a short drive from Ashbury?'

'Well, yeah. With a bit of work. But you are married to the right man for that.'

'I know! If Jim could organise the renovation, maybe Uncle John might not charge us too much rent. We could keep the flat and rent it out. Shall we have another look at the nursery?' The two of them moved off together, pushing a pathway through waist-high weeds. Behind her, she heard Jim's voice:

'Face it, mate. Resistance is useless.'

CHAPTER SEVEN

18 weeks: You might feel your baby move for the first time. She has well formed limbs and may be kicking and punching, as well as sucking her thumb.

The Gatehouse garden had been strimmed to the roots and was full of Sarah and Jim's furniture. Sarah watched as Jim's Mum, Pat, came out of the French windows into the July heat with a duster in her hands, but then couldn't remember what she had gone to get it for. Casting around her, she bumped the back of her calves and ended up sitting on the sofa. 'Dozy mare!' Bob's cackle came from one end of a table he and Jim were shifting across the garden. 'Cheeky sod!' she called back. 'It's just as well you haven't got neighbours, Sarah – we'd lower the tone!'

Sarah stood holding a lamp. On Pat's insistence, they weren't letting her lift a finger, although she was only four months pregnant and full of energy. And this was going to be her home, wasn't it? Pat kept muttering that it was in the back of beyond; she hoped they hadn't bitten off more than they could chew.

'That's it, Mother, sit yourself down,' Jim said. 'Where you going, Dad? Here's fine.'

'Hark at him!' Bob put the table down and wiped dusty hands on his trousers. 'Thinks he's lord of the bleedin' manor! I'll take that, love.' He took the lamp from Sarah. 'Where's this manor house, then?'

'Through the woods, that way.'

'Have they got good fences?' Pat asked.

'Why?' said Jim. 'Because it's a loony bin?'

'A clinic!' said Sarah.

'Stop fretting, will you, Pat?' said Bob. 'I keep saying, it'll be one of these modern things. All group therapy and rich people trying to get off drugs.'

He plonked himself down on the sofa beside her, then Jim sat down on the other side, squashing them all in on the little two-seater. They stretched out their legs in front of them and laughed.

'Come and join us, Sarah!' Pat called.

'Actually, if I'm not allowed to do anything, I think I'll go and explore'.

'Will she be all right?' she heard Pat say as she came to the gate in the wall at the end of the garden. Since Jim first took her home, they seemed to have viewed her as a delicate creature. 'You're like a slim little elf next to us Mercers,' Pat had said. 'We're all big-boned, with a bit of meat on us!' Jim had confided afterwards that they'd all said how posh her accent was.

'We just need the telly,' Bob said as Sarah closed the gate behind her, and more earthy laughter rang out. Soon though, their hilarity was muffled, and she was enveloped by the twittery hush of the woods. As she walked through the cooler, leaf-shaded air, she felt a fluttering movement from the baby.

If there had once been a path, it was completely overgrown, and she was soon battling thick, thorny undergrowth. She was forced to keep changing direction to avoid larger bushes and fallen trees as she made for the unseen compass point of the manor house. She could hear nothing now from the Gatehouse to tell her which way she had come. It couldn't be much further, surely?

Some time later, she found the path blocked by a huge bush with shiny, dark leaves. A sudden crackling sound made her whip her head round. *What's that?* Just trees and fraught stillness in the greenish light. She turned back to the bush and began to force her way through, pushing branches aside. They whipped into place again behind her.

On the other side was a fence made from dry-looking chestnut posts and rusted wire; nothing like the strong ones Jim had seen near the road. She stepped forward and pushed at a post. It leaned over without much resistance.

'What are you doing?' A voice spoke, startlingly close. A man was on the other side of the fence, wearing a dark grey jacket in all this heat. It was his stare that reminded her of the wedding day. It was her uncle. But for a split-second after his brusque challenge, she doubted herself.

'Oh… it's Sarah. I just came for a walk. We're moving in at the Gatehouse.'

He seemed to come to himself. 'Of course… Be my guest.' He inclined his head without taking his eyes off her. 'Well, do let me know if you need anything.' Then he turned and walked away. A little way off he paused and half-turned towards her. 'Welcome home,' he said, before continuing on his walk.

Sarah stared at his retreating back, the blood beating in her ears. It wasn't how she had imagined their second meeting. In fact, what had she thought when she'd first seen him standing there? But he'd been nice then, hadn't he? It was all the silly family talk about fences. She should go back through the woods to the cheerful company in the garden. But part of her wanted to stay and call him back.

Jim smoothed his palms over Sarah's hips through the soft jersey fabric of her dress. He could feel the warmth radiating from her pregnancy in his own middle; reawakening his morning hard-on. But his travel bag and briefcase stood beside them on the quarry tiles, which meant another bloody site visit for Lawsons.

If only he could give up the day job at the building contractors. He had to find that one big property deal that would make his fortune. Last year, he'd bought a Victorian semi from a divorcing couple. When they sold, the local school was in special measures, but now a new management team was turning things round, and there were plans for a new shopping centre nearby. If Jim spent a bit, he could make the house into a desirable residence in an up-and-coming area. But even that wouldn't be the game-changer; the deal those property developers of his had waxed lyrical about, waving their pints, when he was just a labourer with big ideas who went drinking with them.

'Will you be OK?' he asked. When they moved in, she had gone on unpacking until her face was a waxy mask of exhaustion.

'Of course. I'll either be at work or sorting out this place the whole time.'

'I wish you'd let –'

'Jim, I want to do it. I don't want your renovation people ripping it all apart.'

'What do you mean? You loved what they did at the flat.'

'That was different. It belonged to strangers before us.'

He sighed, and looked around him as they headed into the hall. 'There's so much they could do... Skim of plaster, bit of fresh paint...'

'Is this place edging into your fantasy property portfolio?'

'Like other men have fantasy football teams?' Incredible, how she saw straight through to what gnawed at him. It was great that they paid no rent – but he was used to the fenced-off fact of legal ownership; living there as family didn't carry the same clout. Families fell out, didn't they? 'I just want us to make our mark here,' he said.

'I know.' She was gazing at the banisters. She had had to let him strip the paint off them for her because of the toxic chemicals. Now she wiped at a tiny area of the wood like a forensic expert, examining the place for clues. 'But I want it to be our home, not a project. Does it feel like a real home to you?' He put his bags down and wound his arms around her from behind, his chin on her shoulder.

'Of course it does, you nutcase.' He made his voice low and sinister. 'Watch out, or I'll have you carted off to the loony bin across the woods.'

She twisted round to face him. 'You'd better cart yourself off, wide boy. I've got decorating to do.'

'All right. But don't go mad, promise? David said he'd come over and help.'

'Joe knows more about decorating than David!'

'I know that, but Joe was busy. Something about play school. Seriously...'

'I'll lie on the sofa being girly and pathetic until you get back.' She looked anything but pathetic as she tugged her dress into place after his gentle mauling; the pale grey made her eyes look a cornflower blue. He landed a kiss on the flesh over her cheekbone and breathed in the salty scent of her before picking up his bags to go.

The trees stood dead still as he headed for the car. The quiet still surprised him after the peopled hum of the city. They hadn't seen the uncle, or any neighbours, in the weeks since they moved in. Andrew Lovett was still their main contact, and they had had to ask his permission at every stage of the decorating. 'You won't be adding an enormous satellite dish, I hope?' he had said. Probably not even joking. You came across people like him in the property business – they knew nothing about Jim's flair for tasteful, in-keeping conversions; they just heard his accent and took him for some ignorant chav.

Sarah was more at ease with Lovett. She had quizzed him about the history of the Gatehouse. It was funny – she had never been interested in the whole ancestry thing before. But they got home from work one evening to find that that he had dropped off a couple of printed pages from the History Society, and she read them to Jim as if they were the next clue in a treasure hunt.

The Woodlands manor house was built in 1805 for James Briers, who had made his money as a banker to merchants in cotton and silk. The tower was added at the request of his wife, Mathilda; a lover of gothic fiction. The Gatehouse was built in 1806. At that time it was close to the main road to Ashbury; it was a change in the road layout for the building of an industrial estate in the 1970s that left it remote and unconnected to the modernisation of the town. The family's prosperity declined in the later part of the 19th century, along with that of the India merchants, and the bank was eventually sold off. Laurence Briers, born in 1897, was a lawyer rather than a banker. He refurbished the manor house extensively during the 1930s, and this left him with considerable debts. His son Edward was born in 1922.

In 1942, the house was requisitioned as a military hospital. Edward qualified as a doctor and later as a psychiatrist. In 1951 at the age of 29, he married Louise, aged 19, and they had John and Mary. When Laurence died in 1953, Edward decided to turn the manor house into a private asylum, seeing the need for trauma care after the war. In 1954, Woodlands Hospital opened and the Briers family moved into the Gatehouse, which had previously housed the gardener of the estate.

The following day, Sarah phoned Lovett. 'I wanted to find out about my Mum and Uncle John's time,' she told Jim. 'But Andrew only moved here fifteen years ago. He just knows what's in the records, and what the locals have said. He was hoping I could tell him more.' She went quiet, staring at the printout as if trying to decipher a code.

Jim looked back at the weathered sandstone. What would he do if he could have his way here? Put in a new bathroom and kitchen, in keeping with the age and style of the estate. There was that Belfast sink he had seen at an architectural salvage place. Wooden or granite worktops. Reopen the bedroom fireplaces. Strip out all signs of the seventies modernisation, and install a wood-burning aga. *Satellite dish, my arse.* The BMW bumped along the woodland path. How would you go about improving the road access if you owned the place? The scent of a big project surged through him, the pros and cons and possibilities piling up in his mind like an internal file. He shook his head, catching himself. You're getting way ahead of yourself, mate.

'But you must remember something about her?' Sarah looked up from the bottom of the ladder and was confronted by her brother's flat backside in paint-splattered trousers.

'Nope, like I said. Nothing.'

She jabbed at the faded seventies wallpaper with the corner of her scraper. It was hard to remove without bringing the fragile plaster showering down with it, and their progress was slow. The nursery smelled of dust and old paper, dampened with steam, and her scalp tightened as her hair crinkled at the roots.

'What about starting school? Everyone remembers that. She must have taken you, didn't she?'

'I've no idea.' He was meant to be loosening the paper with the steam stripper so that she could scrape it, but he was working way above her head, nudging at barely an inch at a time. She pulled, frustrated, at a dry flap, and a great swathe came away with a gratifying rip. Underneath was a browned, faded nursery pattern showing bunnies wearing clothes.

'Well, when she died, then? You must remember that.'

He pressed the steam stripper against the wall with a resounding clack. 'Why? You don't.' He flicked a glance at her. 'Do you?'

'No. But I was only four. You were six!' She picked at the torn edge of wallpaper around the exposed patch, but it seemed more firmly attached here, as if she had ripped the raised centre off a blister. 'Well, I don't remember it any more than you do.'

She jabbed at the wall in the middle of the bunny paper, suddenly back in their childhood, when he won every argument and chose every game, keeping all the best parts for himself. Metal jarred against plaster with a Jew's harp's musical *bong*, and a whole section crumbled to the floorboards in a shower of rubble and dust.

The heavier particles had settled at her feet before David spoke. 'I – didn't realise we were going back to the brick?'

'Well, looks like we are.' She carried on, making noisy, destructive digs at the wall. Eventually tiredness made her step back, pushing a fist into the small of her back to release a tightening ache. The wall was a crazy pattern of the two different papers and pitted plaster. 'Oh my God, David, look. What a mess.'

He stomped down to the floor and stood beside her. 'Shi-it. You should call that show – what is it, *Decorating Disasters?* In tonight's programme, Help, We've Buggered The Wall.' She slumped on to a rung of the stepladder, tasting plaster, blinking grit from under her eyelids. 'It'll be fine,' he said. 'We can fill in the cracks and paper over it.' But that was rubbish. The room looked like something so wrong that it could never be fixed.

That evening there was an overheated ripeness in the scent of the woods, and ants flew in the last slanting sunlight, heralding an August storm. Sarah stood with arms folded watching David get in his car. It was stupid to feel so knotted up against him as if she hadn't got her way. Waving as he drove away, she saw the ivied housefront reflected in the car's rear windscreen, distorted and dark. She'd wanted him to go before, but now she faced a night on her own.

Soft light spilled from the nursery; nothing like the cold glare of the bulb she had switched off earlier. Sarah pushed at the door with her fingertips. Inside, the wallpaper was clean and new, with vibrant flowers glowing from the chocolate brown. Two little beds were covered in a jumble of toys. The door swung further.

There stood Mary, blue-eyed and wavy-haired. She wore a white nightdress and a tender smile, and she reached out a hand. But then her brow tightened and her smile faltered. She was unsteady – a wobbling animation. Sarah looked down at her mother's feet. She was floating, inches off the floor. A scream tore Sarah's throat.

She clutched at Jim in the bed beside her – but no, he wasn't there. Hot and damp, she pushed the duvet off her. When she sat up, though, the air in the bedroom was cold.

Her bladder clenched in discomfort, but the dream was a lingering presence. *Don't think of it.* She got up, crossed the bedroom, turned on the hall light, and looked quickly both ways. Darkness pressed at the edges of the light-span, filled with the rustling breath of the woods. For a moment, she was afraid to move. *You have to go, or you won't sleep.*

She moved along the corridor, every creak and shuffle jolting her. She turned to check the dark expanse behind her. Nothing. When she looked towards the bathroom, she saw the steps leading up to the locked attic door.

CHAPTER EIGHT

Kim Saunders struggled to unlock the tower room door while clutching a plastic water jug. Her legs and back were one wincing ache, and she should be going off duty now, but Mel had asked her to do this, as she had forgotten. 'Well, it's easy to miss that room, stuck up there.'

Kim was having unchristian thoughts. Mel's subtle slights had made her feel unwelcome ever since she started at Woodlands. Now she kept asking for favours as though they were friends. She caught herself, prodding at resentment – she should forgive, and do this willingly. Soon though, her teenagers would be sloping into the kitchen, asking what was for tea; it was the best time of day for sharing a bit of their lives, albeit mumbled and incoherent. Amy was so listless lately – perhaps she needed to talk.

The door swung open at last. Across an expanse of brown lino, a woman patient sat stiffly in a chair, staring out of a barred window. She was ashen, thin and hunched forwards, with wild hair sticking up around her head. Kim's glance took in a second chair and a small table, a hospital bed, a cupboard and a tiny sink. She walked into the fusty, old-building smell.

'Hello, Mrs Gray, I'm Kim. I'm looking after you tonight. Do you mind if I call you Jane?' Jane's eyes didn't flicker from their fixed point in the treetops beneath the tower. 'Oh she doesn't talk,' Mel had said when Kim asked for her name.

A draught from a half-inch gap under the door chilled Kim's ankles. She reached out to put a hand on an ancient radiator: it was on but wasn't giving out much heat. She put the water down on the table next to an empty jug. Beside it was a soup bowl with a dried-up tidemark over congealed orange leftovers.

Kim unhooked the clipboard from the bottom of the bed. 'Ah, no tablets until later, Jane. It says you're having your treatment with Mr Briers tonight. All right?'

The shadow of a frown – or perhaps just a tic – passed over the woman's brow. She raised a slow hand and held it suspended for a moment, as if the reason for the gesture had been forgotten. Then she pushed at her tangle of hair, like someone patting an elegant hairdo into place. In that Spartan room! Kim had to look away.

'Well. Let's see if we can tidy things up in here. Make it nicer for you.' She pulled back the bedding. The sheet underneath was crumpled and smelt of unwashed skin. Kim turned to the cupboard and pulled down fresh blankets and sheets. 'We'll soon have you more comfortable.'

The room was functional, she told herself, but seemed to have missed out on the modernisation that had taken place downstairs. She found herself thinking of the grim, old-fashioned hospital she had been rushed to as a child, when her sister had drunk a bottle of Codeine Linctus. Overlooked in the panic, Kim had glimpsed patients on trolleys and thought they might be dead. She also remembered nightmarish medical equipment with pumps, bellows and straps. She tucked in the final corner of the blanket and turned.

Jane was putting on lipstick with a shaking hand. It was the dark red of dried blood, and the effect, on her pallid cheeks, was ghastly. Kim went to crouch beside her chair and took her hand.

'Are you making yourself look nice, Jane – for your treatment?' The pale blue eyes stared bleakly ahead.

'Don't take it personally.' Kim leapt to her feet, wrenching unfamiliar muscles. The Director was standing in the doorway. 'That she doesn't chat back. She hasn't spoken for years. Decades, in fact.' He was looking at Kim with a half-smile. 'You're not the usual nurse.'

'No, I'm covering for Mel.' How quiet it was up here; you could hardly hear the sounds of the drugs round or the orderlies' trolleys bustling through the rest of the building. Kim gathered up the empty plastic jug and soup bowl to prove – to him or to herself? – that she was finishing her job and leaving in her own time. 'Well Jane, I'll leave you now. Mr Briers is here for your treatment.'

She glanced back from the doorway. Jane sat staring at the floor, the dark lipstick like a gash across her face. Kim thudded down the spiral staircase, almost losing her footing once in the chill sandstone dimness.

When she finally got home, Kim plonked herself down on the sofa.
'You're home!' she said.

Tom was slumped in an armchair with his feet up on the coffee table, engrossed in a noisy game. He gave her a withering look and she remembered that she had grounded him that morning because she had found him leaning out of his bedroom window, smoking. 'Oh. Yes. I have to say that doing your homework would have looked a bit more penitent.' He shrugged. At sixteen, he was taller than her; it was a relief that he had obeyed her at all and given up his usual after-school routine of hanging around the shopping centre with his mates. 'Look,' she said. 'I'm sorry I went off on one this morning. It just eats away at me, you doing something that could give you cancer. I mean, I bloody breastfed you!'

'In case you hadn't noticed, I'm not actually a baby any more.'

'No. Clearly. I mean, look at the size of your feet!' Kim batted at his enormous school shoes and he paused his game and brought his feet down onto the floor. 'Let's not fight, Tom, I'm too exhausted. Where's your sister?'

A movement of his eyebrows indicated upstairs. 'What's up with her anyway?'

'I don't know. She is quiet, isn't she? But I think she's sick of me asking what's wrong.'

Tom flung his controller onto the sofa. 'Well, if it's someone at school bothering her, she should let me know. I'll sort them out.'

'Oh Tom, that's good of you. But she just keeps saying it's nothing.' They both stared at the TV screen, where a fiery explosion was frozen in time. After a moment, Kim hauled herself to her feet. 'I'll get started on the tea.' The game noise began again as she headed for the kitchen.

The receptionist, in her tailored white uniform, was hair-tossing and laughing with a passing doctor as John Briers began his rounds the next morning. She was very young – like the schoolgirls in town with their bouncing, swaying walk; skirts barely covering their backsides and hair flying above their heads like a flag. She stood at the gleaming island of the reception desk and handed him his mail; her white fingernails surely fake, like her eyelashes and suntan. His finger brushed the springy flesh of her palm, and he caught a quick shrinking look in her eyes.

He walked away, shuffling through bank statements, circulars from medical bodies and an invoice from CareCorps, the nursing agency. As the decor around him became older and the lighting dimmer, he heard muffled grunts and then a hysterical cry.

Two male nurses, one a hefty body-builder type, were pushing a grey-faced youth back into a room. They looked bored and irritated with the exertion.

'No, no, don' make me, no, no.'

'Sorry, sunshine. Those are the rules.' The big nurse gave the youth a decisive shove, and he flew backwards into the room, his gown flapping around scrawny white thighs. The nurses followed and the door swung to. Briers drew level with it as he opened a handwritten envelope. There was a printed card inside.

SARAH AND JIM MERCER HAVE MOVED TO: THE GATEHOUSE, WOODLANDS ESTATE, NR. ASHBURY, KENT.

There were phone, mobile and email details. From the room came a wailing, punctuated by sobs, then the door banged shut. He turned the card over and found neat handwriting on the back:

Dear Uncle John,
We have settled in at the Gatehouse, thank you very much. Sorry to bother you, but I wonder if you have the key to the attic? Hope to hear from you soon.
Regards, Sarah

John Briers stood still. He had seen her that day by the perimeter fence: the image of Mary, as though time had moved backwards and undone everything, and his sister's youth, vitality and innocence were all restored.

He put the card in his jacket pocket. The wailing reached a shrill crescendo and abruptly stopped.

CHAPTER NINE

21 weeks: You might begin to feel more energetic, healthy and positive. Your nesting instinct is probably strong and you will be happiest in your home environment.

Sarah awoke from some deep, helpless place; she had sunk into slack-jawed sleep on the sofa in the early evening. She was abruptly alert and dry-mouthed. What had woken her?

Woodland debris rushed and smattered against the window from the blackness outside. She pulled herself upright, a dragging ache in her hips. Her book clomped to the floor, open at a colour photograph of a baby in the womb. The wind, gusting, aggressive, hushed all other sound. But then a creak. Her mind went to lurid anecdotes that Deb's stepsister, Hilary, liked to drop from her police work. Don't go there. She stretched for the TV remote.

A harsh ringing shrilled through the house. Sarah started so violently that she banged a shin on the coffee table. She got up and limped into the hallway, her skin feeling split, the bone smarting. The porch light threw crazy, tossing shadows on the walls. Through the door glass, a dark shape loomed. *What will you do when Jim's away?* She could pretend she wasn't there – but the bell rang again in rebuke. She crept up to the door and put the chain on, then pulled it a few inches open.

Her uncle stood in the gap, in a dark coat. 'Sarah. You wrote to me, about a key.'

'Oh, of course. Oh, I'm sorry.' She shut him out while she clattered the chain free, then pulled the door wide. His gaze was warming to a smile. She was suddenly aware of the bright pink slipper socks she had put on against draughts, and Jim's old hoodie over her discreet maternity jeans. 'Come in! Please, come in.'

A gust of leaves came skittering in with him, and she rushed to shut out the hectic night. He was staring up at the hallway around them.

'Well. I haven't been here for a very long time.'

'The decorating is a work in progress. Jim's away a lot for work, but my brother, David, has helped me.' Her uncle was very quiet as they toured the house – it was making her rattle on. Of course he knew who David was; he'd have known him before she was born. In the upstairs hallway, a loose floorboard wobbled and she grabbed at the handle of the nursery door to steady herself.

The light she snapped on revealed pitted, chalky plaster, criss-crossed with new grey filler. He stared at torn curls of wallpaper on the floor.

'This is our latest project. Jim will say we should have got decorators in, but I wanted to do it myself.'

'And is it bringing back memories?'

'Oh! No. My first memories are of our house with Dad. No, I was too young I suppose.'

'You don't remember anything at all?'

'No.'

'Well. Perhaps that's for the best.'

She had lost her train of thought. She pushed at a shred of wallpaper with her toe. 'Anyway – DIY's not my forte, but I'm getting there. I'm keen to get the nursery finished, because...'

'You're the image of her. Of Mary.'

She sat down hard on a rung of the stepladder. 'Am I? No one has ever said! I don't really know anything about her.'

'Your father didn't talk about her?'

She shook her head. 'Never.'

'Well. I am surprised at Michael...' He raised an eyebrow, but wearily, as though he shouldn't have been surprised at all.

A wave of heat went through her. 'Well... I suppose it's understandable…'

'Hm. But a shame, for you.'

'Yes.' Was it understandable? Old explanations seemed to wither and lose their grip. 'Were you close? You and my mother?'

He had begun to pace around the room's echoing space. 'We were inseparable.' He caressed the scarred plaster with his palm. 'Well, being twins.'

'Twins? I didn't know!'

'Oh yes. I don't think there is any closer bond.' He had reached the old cupboard with its faded painting of the manor house, and parted the doors gently with his fingers.

'Was this your bedroom? Yours and Mary's?'

'Yes. Our own little world. Our refuge.' He moved to look out through the window bars; his reflected face a hollow-eyed mask in the black. 'Our parents were very busy. We only had each other, really.' He came to lean on the top of the stepladder, which creaked beneath her thighs.

'Did you – bring the key?'

For a while, there was no response. She began to wonder if he had heard. Then there was a shifting and a chink of metal. A ring was dangling in front of her face. Swinging from it was an old-fashioned key.

The camping lantern stood on the attic floor. Under the sloping beams were hulking shapes covered in dust sheets, casting towering shadows. For a moment the only sounds were the hissing of the lantern gas and the wind-haunted trees. Sarah stooped and pulled at the corner of a sheet. Shadows shifted and two spiders ran out in different directions. She turned to look at her uncle and he nodded as though to grant her access.

The sheet was caught. She gave it a great tug and it jerked loose and landed at her feet in a choking cloud of dust. Flapping a hand and peering, she made out two antique trunks. She pulled the lantern closer, knelt in front of one and fumbled to unfasten its clasps. They resisted until she found the precise motion needed, then sprang open together and bruised her thumbs.

'That's it!' Sarah could feel his breath at the back of her neck. Eyes smarting, she lifted the lid and found dozens of loose photographs. She buried her hand in them and began to lift them out one at a time.

A twin boy and girl stood in school uniform, with formal smiles.

And here they were again, in the Gatehouse garden, and here in a school photograph, posed side by side. Now they were young adults, picnicking among sand dunes with sixties hairstyles. Sarah had a mad desire to throw pictures in the air, like someone in a film finding riches, but when she reached further down, she found albums underneath. She opened one. An inscription label with handwriting faded to a coppery purple said: 'The wedding of Mary Briers and Michael Greaves, June 1971'.

Dad was impossibly young and thin, in tight-waisted flares. He stood very upright in his suit and wide purple tie. And beside him was Mary, dark hair falling in ringlets to her shoulders; her white dress slim and elegant with a puffed skirt and gauzy sleeves. On the other side of her was another young man.

'Is that you?' Uncle John nodded, his face in shadow. Had the photographer taken too long, Sarah wondered? Because Mary and John's faces were sombre; only Dad was smiling.

A loose picture caught her eye: Mary with a baby on her lap, and beside her, a sullen toddler. Sarah had never seen her baby head with only downy blond hair before, or David's fair curls and wide-eyed, round face, pouting as he leaned on his mother's knee. Mary looked out at her, young and serious, her baby in the crook of a thin, protective arm. Sarah stared at her eyes, her brows and lips and hairline. Her voice came out tight.

'I always searched Dad's face, and David's. But I never saw...'

'Yourself? It is striking, the resemblance.'

She held onto the photograph. In the other trunk, she found school exercise books marked in childish handwriting: *Mary Briers,* filled with pencilled stories and pictures in wax crayon. *I had Ribeca and Jill rownd to tee. We plad dolls in the nersry. John wos not alowd.* A large jewellery box opened to reveal a tangle of bright and lovely things.

She could have spent hours going through it all, but more shapes were hunched in the shadows, still shrouded in sheets. She began to move between them, wrenching off coverings; heat and dust prickling the pores of her face. A huge moth was unleashed from the darkness and crashed into the lantern, fizzling and batting, casting jagged shadows.

Sarah found furniture and rails of clothes and shoes. On a tailor's dummy was the wedding dress from the photograph, standing out in the lamplight from the murky dark. She reached out to touch it, but noticed a tear between the bodice and skirt, and drew back, afraid to damage it further. A full-length mirror showed strange shadows on her face, and her pupils black and huge. Uncle John was behind her, reaching out a hand. Oh, he was picking a cobweb from her hair. She tucked back a curl and left a streak of dirt on her cheek.

'I look like a madwoman! Sorry. I wanted to see all of it at once.'

'Of course. That's only natural.'

Behind him on the corner of a chest of drawers, she spotted a dark wooden statue. It stood a foot high and showed a pregnant woman with long, slim legs, standing on a circular base. She went and picked it up. It was heavy, and the wood was cool and smooth to the touch. 'This must have been my mother's. Would it be OK to take it downstairs?' He looked distracted. Of course, he didn't know – she had hoped she'd have a chance to tell him in person. She felt huge, but if she was wearing certain clothes, people still didn't notice. She smiled at the swollen wooden belly, a hand going to her own. 'I'm expecting a baby in December.'

John crashed back through the buffeting darkness, the sweet nostalgia of earlier in the evening gone. This same walk then had been thick with memories; this path, now so overgrown, he and Mary had trodden together since they were small. He had even used the same hole in the fence, concealed by the bush. It had been their secret, since they were not allowed in the grounds of the clinic, where Father looked after his mad people.

Then Sarah had opened the door to him and shown him the room where he and Mary had spent their childhood. He could almost see her again, bustling about the nursery with her silly little friends, praising and scolding her dolls and teddies. Later, of course, the friends fell away and he had her to himself.

How bewildering to stand in the cramped, lamplit attic, among Mary's belongings, inches from the warm, living reminder of what was lost.

But then her news, dropped smiling, with her hand on her belly, clutching the statue like the winner of an award. He stumbled to a stop now beside the laurel bush that hid the opening in the fence. He was out of breath and his ankles stung from forcing his way through brambles; one arm felt bruised where he had batted aside a branch. She must wonder why he had left so abruptly when they were getting on so well. He stood in the dank leaf-mould; chill wetness seeping through his shoes. Ridiculous, storming through the woods like an overwrought child.

He had stalked across to Woodlands to find Father, and tramped through a wilderness of corridors, practising the questions he was meant to ask. People turned and stared, but they wouldn't help him; he wasn't allowed here. How could you be sure which were the mad ones? He covered miles and miles of corridor at a frantic trot. By the time he found the right office, his face was screwed up, his nose filling with snot.

'What do you think you're doing here? What's got into you?'

'I just...' His chest heaved, his lips pulled back. 'We just wanted... to ask you... We want... We just want Mummy...' He hadn't meant to sound such a baby.

'You are not allowed to come here. And you can't have your mother. Now stop that silly noise!' But the noise wouldn't stop, it was coming from a knot in his chest. His father took him by the arm and shook him: 'Are you a girl, crying like that? Should I get you one of Mary's skirts?' He dragged him from the room with his arm yanked high.

'No. No!' He choked down the crying as they swept along, but it left him shuddering. Father stopped near an outside door and let go of his arm.

'Forget about her. Do you hear me? And get back home.' He stumbled across the grounds and through the woods, clutching the hurt place on his arm. But it was no use; there was only Mary there – Mummy had gone.

CHAPTER TEN

Hilary was in the kitchen of the witness's house, making tea with her fellow officer DC Amal Jafri when Deb called with the plan for Joe's party. The tea was, as ever, an excuse to give everyone a break from the gruelling subject at hand.

'I might have to swap a shift…' Hilary said, then whispered to Amal with a look of appeal, 'It's my stepsister, about my nephew's party'. Amal had a big, extended family and knew the importance of these events. Sure enough, he rolled his eyes, but nodded. 'Yes, that's sorted. I'll be there.'

'Are you sure?'

'Well I'm not going to miss it, am I?'

'OK. You all right? Have I caught you at a bad time?'

'We're with a victim. Just having a tea break to help everyone to chin up and soldier on. Send me a prezzie list will you?'

When she ended the call, Amal was standing ready with three mugs on a tea tray. He inclined his head towards the living room. She made a *Ready as I'll ever be* face and they went back in.

Gareth had seemed quite self-possessed at the beginning of the interview, a bulky fifty-five-year-old straining against the shirt and suit trousers of a salesman. An hour and a half in, he had been quivering and struggling to make sentences. His shirt, Hilary saw as they resumed, was blotted with damp.

'I know it's hard, Gareth,' she said. 'But – for the statement, can you tell me where he made you put your hand next?' Gareth wiped his face and looked at the sweat on his fingers. Hilary was probably young enough to be his daughter, if he had ever had a child. She knew from months of talking to him that he had never even managed a relationship. He stuttered out more detail, interrupted by Amal requesting clarifications with the bald anatomical terms of a biology lesson. He sounded callous, but she knew that he wasn't. When the going got tough, Amal got crisp and professional.

'And where did he touch you?' Hilary asked. Gareth's living room felt stale and airless, his distress hanging in the air like an odour. He seemed about to answer, but it was a startling noise that burst from his throat. Still, they couldn't leave it there – they had to push onwards. Gareth told them the really nasty stuff in a strangled whine, as if a tormented little boy was buried in all that adult flesh.

'Fuck,' she said in the patrol car afterwards. 'Forty years later, and he couldn't talk about it without retching.'

'I know,' Amal replied. 'Fuck.'

They didn't say much on their way back to the station, but when they pulled up outside, Hilary sat back in the driving seat. 'Remind me why I do this?'

She had always wanted to be a police officer, but couldn't think of a single bright hope that hadn't been trampled on in the last couple of hours. She switched the radio on and turned it up when she heard a song she liked, ignoring Amal's grimace. She had been ten when she went round to feed their neighbours' cat while they were on holiday. She had found the back door broken, drawers pulled out and belongings strewn on the floor. Hilary had managed to get home without breaking into a run and had struggled to make herself heard over the family's morning noise. 'Listen, Mum!' Deb had called on her behalf when she saw her face. For once, what she said was not treated as cute but silly. The police officers who came praised her lack of alarm, her clear announcement of the facts. She watched them from her bedroom window, speaking into their walkie talkies in language like a code, and longed to examine the crime scene with them.

'It'll make a difference,' Amal said quietly, so that she had to turn the music down, 'to people like Gareth, who no one has ever listened to.'

He was right, wasn't he? They had spent months building this historical abuse case against Ashbury's prestigious private school. The victim statements were piling up while the town went about its business, largely unaware of the devastation that some of its most esteemed citizens had caused. Gareth had been a scholarship boy, the proudest achievement of his parents, who had worked two jobs each to pay for his uniform and school trips. They never understood why this privileged start in life had failed to be the making of him.

It had taken Gareth forty years to tell them.

The news came on. Hilary grabbed her briefcase and was about to head inside, but Amal put a hand on her arm and nodded towards the radio. A similar case in the north of England had collapsed in court. They looked at each other as the words rang round the car: *Justice Stephen Brennan was highly critical of the Department of Public Prosecutions for putting the defendant through a trial at huge cost to the public purse, when the case against him was so flimsy.*

Were there victims like Gareth in that case too? Were their abusers still out there, knowing they'd got away with it?

'Have you heard?' DS Keith Prentice said when they got back to the team's cramped office, known among themselves as the Troll Hole. A row of slit-like windows above head height shed the only natural light.

'About the Preston case?'

'Closer to home,' Keith said from his cluttered desk. 'Two of our witnesses have withdrawn their complaints. They heard about Preston on the news. Which leaves us with nothing against Yates or Hardiman.'

'Shit. We've just spent the last hour watching a grown man cry.'

'The DI says we're still going after Kravitz,' Keith said. 'But how long before that goes tits up, too?'

'But all the witnesses point to him,' Hilary said. 'He was running his own sick little empire of pain.'

'Oh, but such an upstanding pillar of the community... Rotary Club, patron of the arts, best mates with mayors, councillors, police chiefs...'

There were times when Hilary could appreciate Keith's straight-talking realism, but this wasn't one of them. She thought of the things Kravitz, the headteacher, had said publicly about his accusers: that they were losers, fantasists and liars – and pain spiked in her temples.

Amal had picked up a pen. He flung it down. 'I've gotta tell you, I'm getting closer and closer to going back to my cousin about that private investigator thing.'

'Amal! You wouldn't, would you? Who'll keep me awake on

stake-outs?'

'Yeah, and going private – really?' Keith said. 'I thought your dream was to join the SAS.'

'We've got a baby on the way though, haven't we? Time for dreaming's over.'

The files at Hilary's elbow might as well have been piled up on her chest. 'But don't you want to see this through? At least try to nail Kravitz after all this bloody work?'

Amal shrugged. 'Of course I do.' But he didn't look convinced.

CHAPTER ELEVEN

'I'm not being funny,' Stephanie, the East Wing staff nurse said, 'but I know you like the hours here and it's convenient for you. So, if I were you, I wouldn't ask too many questions.'

'Right,' Kim replied. 'Right. What – sorry, I'm not sure what you mean?'

Stephanie kept her eyes on the trolley that they were loading up for the drugs round. 'It's just – they have a certain way of doing things here. They don't like it questioned.'

Who had been talking about her? Surely not Reverend Benson, the elderly chaplain? He had nodded, frowning, when Kim told him what was troubling her, and said, 'You see, I sense that people are at peace here. But your compassion is commendable. Keep praying.'

'Is this about Jane Gray in the tower? Because, I just needed to know what I was dealing with.'

She had been unable to get Jane out of her mind. The other nurses said she had been there for years. She never spoke, though no one knew whether she had some physical problem or was an elective mute. One of the older orderlies remembered her 'screaming blue murder' when she was first brought in. Despite the neglected air of the tower room, she was treated by the Director himself. There were rumours that she was an important person whose identity was kept secret; perhaps even minor royalty.

'It's more of a general attitude,' Stephanie said.

'Well, I'm sorry if it comes over like that. Look, Stephanie, I'm no expert – I just did a tiny part of my training in a psychiatric unit. But I did learn a few things, like building relationships with patients, monitoring the results of treatment – even working with families to promote recovery. Some of the patients seem to have been here for years. It's just a concern, isn't it, if they're not getting any better?'

Stephanie wouldn't catch her eye. 'We just do what's asked of us here. Or go elsewhere. Do you see what I'm saying?' She pushed the full trolley out of the pharmacy and along the corridor. Kim followed, her scalp tightening into an ache.

'Yes, I think I do.'

In the kitchen, hours later, Kim was chopping carrots to conceal in pizza sauce. The radio was playing a chatty drive-time show, but her head was still full of that bloody clinic. Tipping the chopped bits into a pan of tomatoes and onions, she saw herself explaining the case against Woodlands to some high-up official. Tabloid headlines. A scandal. An inquiry.

She hauled at the jammed back door, which burst open, shaking the house, and leaned out to snip the last surviving herbs from the patio pots. Stephanie was right: the hours at Woodlands did suit her and the pay was better than most of the work available to her. And yet to go along with it all was to be as bad as the most neglectful nurse at the clinic – or like old Benson, who only saw what he chose to see. But she was a divorced mother with a mortgage to pay; she couldn't afford whistleblower heroics. And yet, Jane… *Lord, tell me what to do, I'm completely clueless,* she prayed, holding handfuls of broccoli under the tap.

When she turned from the sink, Amy was there, peering into the tomato pan.

'Hi darling! All right? Good day?'

Amy shrugged with hunched shoulders. Her hair hung in straightened curtains, concealing all but the middle third of her face.

'I can't believe you still hide carrots in the pizza.' She picked up a wooden spoon and poked at the sauce, one long leg hooked around the other.

'Tom would get scurvy otherwise.' Amy didn't smile. Until recently she had been so cheerful; you knew when she was in the house because you could hear her singing, or chattering on her phone.

'School OK?'

'Fine.' Amy leaned over the worktop, cupping her chin in her hands, all long legs and angles, like a grasshopper. The next moment she shifted again, pulled herself upright and sighed. What might be troubling a thirteen-year-old? Bullying? Anxiety about her appearance? Still the divorce? 'How's the madhouse?' Amy said.

'Fine. Well, not fine. I don't think they help people much there. Remember I told you about Quentin? Who I'd just got to talk to me about his mum? Well they've changed my shifts so I won't see him any more. There's no continuity of care.' Should she be telling Amy something so depressing? On the other hand, they were sharing some version of their day. 'And there's this poor woman, all on her own in a grotty room up in a tower. They say she hasn't spoken for years. But no one knows if she can't or just doesn't. I'd love to help her, but I can't think how.'

'Maybe you can get her to talk.'

Kim saw the barred window, the grey stare, and gave a snort of disbelief, then regretted it for Amy's sake. 'Oh, bless you. I should try, shouldn't I?'

Amy shrugged, but as though it were obvious rather than hopeless. Kim gave her daughter's stiff-limbed body a quick, tight hug and wondered if she felt it relax a little. What happened to the warm, unthinking intimacy of childhood? She went to the fridge and began to rummage for pizza toppings

'When's tea ready?'

'About half an hour. You could get started on your homework.' Amy shuffled out of the kitchen, her school bag bumping on her hip, and Kim called after her in a stage whisper, 'And don't let on about the carrots!'

As she banged the oven door on the pizza, a solution to the work problem came to her. It had seemed insoluble earlier, and the idea appeared to have come from nowhere, when she was thinking of something else. But Kim knew better, and closed her eyes for a second in the yeasty warmth. *Thank you.* She would talk to Mel, who resented going up into the tower, and see whether she could take the task from her. She couldn't fix everything at Woodlands, but she could do this.

CHAPTER TWELVE

22 weeks: You are probably very hungry, and during the next ten weeks, you will put on about half of the weight you gain in pregnancy. Your baby is making white blood cells to help him fight infection and disease.

'You there?' Sarah heard Jim's travel bag thud onto the floor of the hall. 'What was your news?' He appeared in the doorway of the living room, crossed the space between them in quick paces and pulled her into his grasp.

'Missed ya,' he said, his breath warm on her neck.

'You too.' She shifted to loosen him, and swept a hand around her to make him look. The oak mantelpiece had had a minimalist look before, with just one chunky vase in the middle. Now it was crowded with faces. The statue of the pregnant woman stood on the side table by the phone, and albums were piled on the sofa.

'What's all this..?'

'Family things. My uncle came round with the key to the attic.'

'Really? So how did that go?'

'Really well. He was nice. Kind of charming in an old-school way. He hadn't been here for years. He – told me about my mother.' She faltered. They had never really talked about this. What if he didn't understand? But the news was like a tide, heaving inside her, and she began to pour it out.

'They were twins. Can you believe it? I didn't even know that! And it could have been relevant, couldn't it, with the baby? And he said – oh, loads of stuff, about their childhood in the nursery. And then he took me up and showed me the attic.' She glanced at him, watchful in case he edged away, his mind going ahead to the kitchen for a beer. 'Jim, it's all up there, a lifetime's worth of stuff – her school books, clothes, furniture – I'll have to show you. Look, this is my parents' wedding photograph. I framed it. And this statue; she must have got it when she was pregnant. I thought we could have it down here. What do you think?'

'Of course. It's great.' He squeezed her to his side, peering at the wedding photograph. 'It's true, you do look like her.'

She felt herself relax into his shape. 'I haven't asked about your trip. Are you hungry? Shall I get you something?'

'It's fine. I had a sneaky Little Chef.' He put the photograph back in its place. 'You've got a mantelpiece to rival Deb's!'

Sarah looked at the clutter, the faces, where previously she hadn't even allowed Jim to put his keys. She let out a laugh. 'I have, haven't I? She thinks she's got family – we'll that is a family!'

Jim came in later in his bathrobe, glowing from the shower, his hair in spikes. 'I had a look up in the attic.'

'Oh! I was going to show you.'

'I couldn't resist having a butcher's. Oh look, it's my thing, isn't it? Poking round properties? Anyway I don't think you should go up there any more.'

'What? Why?!'

'Keep your hair on. It looks like there's woodworm. I'm not sure the floor is safe.'

'Really? It seemed okay.'

'I think we should get someone to look at it. Just to be sure.' He sat beside her, then slid along the sofa, picked her feet up and put them in his lap. Peeling off a sock, he began to caress and squeeze her sole. Tightness subsided from muscles all over her body. She heard him murmur: 'We don't want you falling through the ceiling, the amount you weigh these days.'

They looked at her bump, standing proud in a clinging top. 'I just had a really big dinner,' she said, fighting off a yawn. She woke up some time later, her feet still in his lap, from a dream that he was blundering through the attic, knocking things over.

'Sarah, it's incredible.' Deb stood beside her the next day, contemplating the pictures on the mantelpiece.

'I know – and there's loads more in the attic. I could spend days up there, just exploring it.' Sarah led the way into the kitchen, where a Welsh dresser displayed a collection of blue and white china milk jugs. The cosy farmhouse feel was completed by an oak table, where another album lay open. 'I'm going through these, trying to work out who everyone is.'

Deb sat down and flipped through the pages while Sarah made tea in a teapot with a pattern of tiny blue flowers, which she had bought from a local pottery. After a moment, the flipping stopped.

'My God, Sarah! She's just you!' Sarah leaned over to see a portrait of Mary. Her brow and upper lip had a strong, echoing shape, and dark hair rose from her hairline and descended into waves and curls. Her friend was looking up into her face. 'You're so different from your Dad and David. And – here's why. She's the missing link.'

'I know. It was the strangest feeling when I first saw her face.' Sarah had looked forward to just such a moment, but as she carried the tea to the table, she felt an absence like a hole letting the cold in. 'Couldn't David come?'

'He actually offered to look after Joe so I could come. I know! I nearly fell off my chair. I think he thought it was women's stuff – you know, family memories...'

Sarah poured their teas. 'I thought he'd be interested. It is his family, too.'

'You know David. Stiff upper everything.'

'I suppose. Oh, Deb, I was high as a kite when I saw it all. I've got these treasures to show the baby one day. But I keep wondering why my uncle hasn't been in touch since. He left really abruptly. Almost as if I'd offended him. Until then he seemed to like me.' She saw Deb's lips twitch and smiled herself. 'Listen to me! Like a teenager talking about some boy! I've only just met him. And I was fine without him before.' She pulled the album on to her lap and slapped it shut. 'He said something weird.'

'What?'

'I told him I didn't remember anything about living here, and he said, *Perhaps that's for the best.*'

For a moment, only the shushing of the trees sounded in the woods overshadowing the kitchen.

'Perhaps what's for the best – that you don't remember anything?'

'I suppose so. Do you think he meant, about her dying?'

'Maybe. Because, however good all the other memories were, there would be that sad one at the end. But you've got all these lovely things now. And I'm sure your uncle will come round again. I bet he's thrilled to have this brilliant, long-lost niece on his doorstep.'

Sarah hugged the album to her chest. 'It seems weird now that I knew nothing about her for so long and hardly thought about it. You know, I don't even know what she died of.'

Jim sat on the leather sofa in Woodlands reception, looking round at the modern fittings moulded to the yawning nineteenth-century hallway. He tried to get a feel for the age of the place, and pictured a hunting party gathering, servants dashing about and hooves clattering outside – he'd probably got the scene from that costume drama Mum was always glued to.

The house smelt of old stone – the whiff of money and power. Where was Briers? His voicemail had brought Jim straight from football without a shower; he hoped the gusty wind had deodorised him before he pulled on his tracksuit and training top. Two nurses padded through, exchanging greetings with the receptionist, who was cute, with that over-painted, Essex-girl look. They looked over at Jim. Shit, did they think he was a patient, sitting here?

A measured tread echoed in the high-arched space; and he turned to see a suited older man approaching.

'Jim?'

'Yes!'

Unsure whether to stand or not, he half-rose and ended up in a silly, crouching handshake.

Briers perched on an armchair a little distance away and undid his jacket button. 'So. I gather you have some questions for me.'

'Yes. Yes, thanks for seeing me. I wondered about the scope of what we're allowed to do at the Gatehouse... For instance, I think there's woodworm in the attic. And we're a bit concerned about the fences between us and the Clinic. They seem to be in some disrepair.' Briers had Sarah's eyes, but with none of their warmth. Jim wouldn't have called him charming. 'Normally, I'd just sort it all out, but I'm a bit unclear about our status as tenants. There's a lot of decorating I'd do if it was allowed. You know, improvements. As I think I told you at the wedding, I'm quite experienced in the property game.'

'Yes, I believe you did mention it,' Briers said. Jim launched into an explanation of his work at Lawsons and his own business achievements. Briers seemed to wait for him to stop, then considered for a time, unhurried.

'You can arrange for woodworm treatment. And decorating, as long as you run everything past Lovett. Our ground staff here maintain the fences. As for your status as tenants – you are welcome to stay at the Gatehouse as family members, rent free, as originally discussed. Who knows, perhaps we'll make a more permanent arrangement in due course.'

Jim looked over the reception area and down a grand corridor stretching into the bowels of the building. He'd expected some minor country squire's house, but this was in a different league altogether. Places like this stuck fast in families, didn't they – hardly ever changing hands. 'Great place you've got here. Very impressive.' Hearing his own words, he hated his ingratiating tone.

'Mm. My father inherited some rather impressive debts with it. He had to turn it into an asylum to make it pay. Which then became my lot.'

'Yeah. Yeah, Lovett said that's when the family moved to the Gatehouse. And later, Sarah and David lived there with their Mum and Dad, didn't they?'

The talk had edged into something more personal. There might be titbits to take home to Sarah, whose excitement after her uncle's visit had now dulled to quiet thoughtfulness.

Briers barely nodded. He made it all sound like a liability, but at the end of the day, he owned this massive pile, didn't he? How much was it worth? With the grounds and the Gatehouse too? An oddity occurred to Jim that he hadn't thought of before.

'But – your father didn't leave it to Mary. The Gatehouse, I mean.' Shit – what was he saying? If Mary had inherited the Gatehouse, it would belong to Sarah and David now. Did it sound like that's what he was after? He was like Mum, rushing in to fill awkward pauses with chatter. Now no one was saying anything. Jim saw the receptionist glance over at them. Should he get up to leave?

'My father didn't trust women much,' Briers said at last. 'Perhaps he was old-fashioned. He decided I would become a doctor and take over from him here. The Gatehouse went with the job. Although, when he thought I wasn't studying hard enough, he used to threaten to leave the whole lot to Battersea Dogs' Home.' He gave a loud, single guffaw. 'Hah!'

Sarah worked on her laptop at the kitchen table, with printouts of the new *Madness* material spread out around her. Eva Leary had sent the extra chapter as an after-thought, and Sarah had been so tied up with checking a book for Rebecca, an editor in her team, that she hadn't had time to read it until this Sunday morning, while Jim played football.

She was distracted by an urgent need for tuna. She opened a can and drained the oil into the sink, hearing Jim: *Kid's going to be born with fins.* He was really late now, even allowing for a drink after the game. She put the meaty fish in a bowl and mixed in mayonnaise and sweetcorn, then crammed a thick layer between slices of granary bread, and sat down to eat over the typescript. As she took in the sobering material, a series of little movements flittered through her womb.

In rare but high-profile cases, Eva wrote, mentally ill people murdered strangers, provoking a media furore and calls for the public to be better protected. Disinformation about conditions such as schizophrenia proliferated, echoing the deep-seated fears of bygone ages.

Sarah's editorial brain suspected a repetition from another chapter and she began to scroll through the onscreen layout, looking for its first appearance. But soon she forgot what she was looking for. 'We must sort out that dodgy bit of fence between us and Woodlands,' Jim had said. 'Especially with the baby coming.' She hadn't exactly disagreed. Were they demonising the mentally ill? Or were there dangerous people at Woodlands?

Beyond the solitary space of the house, her tensed ear caught a distant crackle, rising to a rush. Slam. She started and swore. Footsteps crunched and the front door clattered open.

'Oh my God. You gave me a fright.'

Jim was bright-eyed and dishevelled. 'Sorry!' He planted a kiss; a pale hint of beer on his breath. Veering off to the fridge, he stood within its open door, tipping bottled water straight down his throat.

'Did you win?'

'Lost 3-1. Good game though.'

'Against the run of play, was it?'

'Oh yeah. We had them on the run. I mean all they had over us was the goals.'

'And did you have a big session afterwards to celebrate? I had to eat without you, so I didn't die.'

'Oh – no, just a quick one. I've been to see your uncle.'

'What? What do you mean – you just dropped in on him? Jim?'

'No. I rang.' He sat at the table holding a cold slice of homemade pizza.

'But we don't have a number for him.'

'I rang the clinic a few days ago, got the receptionist and left a message.'

'What message? I can't believe you contacted him. Without telling me.'

'I just wanted to sort out the woodworm and the fences.' He eased the sagging point of the pizza slice between his lips. 'And I didn't want to get your hopes up in case he didn't get back to me. Then after football, I found this voicemail.'

He gave a bald account of his visit, and she darted in with questions to fill in the gaps.

'So – you just wanted his permission about the woodworm?' she asked when he had finished. 'Or do you actually want to buy this house from him? Jim?'

He put his hands up like someone cracking under interrogation. 'All right. It's not like I haven't thought about it...'

'And ... you think he might sell?'

'Well I thought it sounded positive, what he said.'

How had things got this far without her realising he was thinking this way? He always got this focused, engrossed look when he had a property in his sights. Her mind had been completely elsewhere. She stood up to get a drink, but he took her arm and pulled her on to his lap.

'It's weird though, that it's his to sell in the first place.'

'What do you mean?'

'Well – why did he inherit it all? I mean, it was Mary who lived at the Gatehouse.'

'He was the son...'

'But not the oldest son. They were twins. And she had a family. Imagine, if the old man had left it to your Mum, it would be rightfully yours now. Or yours and David's.' She stared at him. 'What?' his arms tightened around her and he gave her a playful shake, jiggling her bottom against his legs.

'You! The way your mind works!'

Jim laughed, moving his hand in her hair. 'I was just making enquiries. Seeing how the land lies. Anyway, I got the answers I was after, and then I came home. To you.'

The racing thoughts he had conjured began to scatter. She felt the motion of his hand, the hard muscles of his thighs beneath her and the warm, tangy scent of him. She started to say something but the words faded to a sighing breath. The next moment they were kissing deeply. 'I'm going to take you upstairs,' he said.

Pregnancy had swelled her blood and heightened every sensation.

She lay in a prolonged reverberation, passion still thrilling through her, even as Jim got up and moved off towards the shower. The black-beamed ceiling looked down on this place where her family had lived its unknown story. Cool air crept over the moisture on her skin, and she pulled the duvet around her in a sudden chill.

The lush greenery of the woods had yellowed in an early cold spell and was shot through with beams of sunlight. It was a couple of weeks since Jim's visit to Woodlands. Nearing home, Sarah recognised the figure in the dark overcoat from a distance, and changed down a gear. It seemed unthinkable to drive past without stopping, but her uncle was with a man in green overalls and was pointing into the undergrowth. He looked up at the sound of her car, but carried on talking. As she drew level, he lifted a hand in greeting. She braked to a halt and got out. The other man began to poke at the hip-high thicket with a stick.

'Hello again,' said Uncle John. 'We're looking at some woodland management issues. This is one of our groundsmen.' The man did not look up, perhaps realising he was being explained rather than introduced.

'Ah! And I'm heading home to see a man about some woodworm.'

'Ah yes. Your husband mentioned it.' They stood and watched the groundsman hauling bramble stalks from a chaotic tangle; the only fruit clinging to them looked shrivelled and dry.

'I hope you didn't mind him coming to see you. He – likes things to be clear.'

'I see. Yes.'

The intimacy of the attic seemed a strange, vivid memory. Perhaps it had been a mistake to stop the car. 'Well. Anyway, thank you for opening the attic for me. It was – really helpful.' She turned to go.

'It must have been a lot to take in.'

'Yes, I... My head has been spinning with – all sorts of questions.'

A clang came from the undergrowth. The groundsman was pulling aside bracken and bramble stalks. Sarah glimpsed dark metal, blistered with blood-bright rust.

'Aha! I knew it must be there,' said Uncle John. The other man's grunting effort uncovered ornate black curls and flourishes – finally revealed to be part of a little wrought-iron bench. 'The picnic bench! Mary and I would sit there and eat little feasts, pilfered from the kitchen. Who would have thought the years could cover it over so entirely.'

His expression was full of pleasure and gave her courage. 'I hope you don't mind,' she said. 'It's just, I've got no one else to ask. As I said before, I know almost nothing about her. I don't even know how she died.'

Her ears had begun to ring in the quiet when he finally replied. 'Sometimes we think we want to know something, but we're better off not knowing.'

'Oh.' He gave a series of nods and she found her head bobbing in return. She said, 'Oh,' again, as though he had explained something.

He touched her arm. 'It's probably best.'

'Well, I'd better get back – for the woodworm man.' She turned away and blinked; her eyes seemed to have filled. She faced him with a smile and nodded again, then got back in the car.

At the house, she found an answerphone message from the woodworm man, cancelling the appointment. She should give in to her leaden afternoon fatigue, and have a rest. But the silence in the house seemed shrill. She headed for the kitchen to make a start on their evening meal, but just stood there; she didn't know how long.

Sarah erupted from the house. Her feet pounded the path; her womb a heavy ache; arms folded across her chest. At the sound of her footsteps, her uncle lifted his head. The groundsman had walked away by the time she reached his side.

'Please tell me,' she said.

CHAPTER THIRTEEN

24 weeks: Your organs have less space as your uterus expands and you may be finding it harder to breathe. Your baby can now open her eyes. A loud noise may make her jump.

They sat on the uncovered iron bench.

'You really don't know anything?' her uncle asked.

'Nothing. I'm sorry but – now I know there's – something – I can't get on with anything. I just have to know. I ...'

'When your mother died,' he cut in, 'she was a mental patient. At Woodlands.' A hush, then a seashore rush of sound: crashing, twigs snapping, squirrels chasing each other through the branches overhead.

'What?' Sarah's voice snagged. 'Why?'

'Well, she was judged to be... a danger to herself and others.'

It made no sense. She had started to think there must have been some awful crime. 'But – why?'

'That, Sarah, I cannot say.' He leaned forward and stood up. 'I'm sorry.'

She pushed up onto her feet. 'Please!' she said, over the nasty chattering of the squirrels. 'You can tell me. I've always been strong about these things. My Dad was very … unsentimental. He never let us feel sorry for ourselves. I'll be OK.'

Leaves fluttered to the ground in silence.

'Your mother tried to smother you with a pillow,' he said. 'In your bed, as you slept. David woke up and screamed for your father. She was taken away, to Woodlands. And then one day she got out of her restraints somehow, and threw herself from the tower.' Mist rose from the tangled earth.

Trees whirled overhead, streaked with light. He was holding her upright, clasping her back and ribs through her coat.

They walked in this way to the Gatehouse. She was on the sofa and he was making her sip water, adding drip on drip to a foul swell of nausea. 'Promise me you'll call Jim,' he said when she insisted the dizziness was better and he should go. But she just sat alone, looking at the cluster of pictures on the mantelpiece: her little family shrine.

A key grated in the lock. 'Hiya!' came a voice, cheerful and alien. 'Sarah? What's the matter? What's happened?' Jim grasped her hands and then shook them when she didn't answer. 'Sarah?'

'My Mum tried to kill me, when I was little. They took her to the clinic. She killed herself.'

'What? Who told you this?'

'My uncle. In the woods. I made him tell me.'

'Shit! That's terrible. I'm so sorry.'

She felt crushed and airless in his embrace, and pulled away. There was a strange look on his face. It took her a moment to recognise it. Relief – that was it, he was relieved. 'I thought, when I saw you … I thought it was the baby,' he said. But relief wasn't right. She was standing still but in her head she kept on falling. *She tried to smother you with a pillow, in your bed, as you slept.*

Later in the evening, Sarah hung tomorrow's shirt from the back of Jim's bedside chair. Movement, agitated and brisk, felt right. His stillness on the bed was an affront. When she reached in her wardrobe, the hangers tangled together. She yanked at them and a blouse slipped and crumpled on the floor.

'Sarah, please. Leave that.'

'We've still got work!' He reached out for her arm as she passed. 'I can't believe no one told me,' she said.

'I suppose you wouldn't tell that to a little girl...'

'But it feels like everything's a lie. Don't you get that? I trusted my Dad. He answered all my questions: where do babies come from? Is God real? Who's right in the argument on telly? He never talked down to me. But it turns out he lied.' She pulled away, hooked the hangers on the back of her chair, and began to sort through the briefcase which stood on the seat. But the things inside were meaningless, and the clasp would not fasten. She gave the chair, briefcase, clothes a great shove and it all fell with a crash to the floor.

'Sarah! Don't!' He made her sit on the bed. 'I know this is terrible for you. I'm sorry. But we've got to calm down.' His voice was so peaceful and sure. She could almost believe in being calm. 'The baby's all right, so we'll be all right. OK? Think of the baby.'

'Don't you think I am thinking of the baby? I'm thinking, what kind of mother is it going to have?'

'A brilliant mother. You'll be brilliant.'

'Jim, people learn from how they were mothered.'

'But look how great you are with Joe. You'll be fantastic.'

Could she believe that? She sank her head against him, too tired suddenly to stay upright. After a moment, she felt him shift gently, and he laid her down, her head finding soft rest in her pillow. When she stayed there, unmoving, he lifted her legs onto the bed, and covered her with the duvet. She was half aware of him moving about, clearing the debris from the floor. Please, let sleep come; make it all stop. But the pillow and the screams ran through her head in a relentless, repetitive loop.

Joe's face was lit by three candles stuck into a chocolate caterpillar. A ragged 'Happy Birthday' rang tunelessly out. Deb's camera snapped, capturing his delight as he blew out the flames in a shower of spit. David had even come down from the attic and was poised with the cake knife, making wry comments to watching parents. Deb tried to catch his eye as the lights came on, to point out Joe, revelling in a round of applause. *Look, David; his little face* – but he was laughing at an aside from one of the dads.

The toddlers were restless, their heads sweaty from party games; faces smeared with food. Hyped up to the point of hysteria. Joe was looking around him in wonder; the big day they had counted down to was here at last. She called out like an impresario, 'Right. Who wants a piece of birthday cake?'

'Me!' 'Meee!!' There were yells and even screams. In the middle of it all, the doorbell rang. Deb locked eyes with Hilary, who looked the coolest of aunties in denim and stripes, a little girl she had barely met wrapped around her leg. Toddlers loved Hilary, perhaps for her restless energy or for her face, which still had a child-like quality.

'Could you get that, Hil?'

'I'm on it!' Hilary managed to unwrap the girl, who ran out after her through a door festooned with streamers. The interruption had broken a spell and the other children began to stand on their chairs, clamber down or whine. Hilary came back in and Deb craned her neck to see who was with her. Sarah was in smart maternity work clothes, but her hair hung at an odd angle from a dangling clip. Her face, unsmiling in the festive confusion, looked wrong.

'Joe, it's Auntie Sarah!' Deb tried in an upbeat tone.

'I need to talk to you,' Sarah said to David, as though no one else were there.

'Me?'

'Daddy, I wanna cake!' shouted Joe. But David handed the cake knife to Deb, and turned to go. Joe stood on his chair and bellowed. 'I wanna cake! I wanna Daddy!' He erupted into screaming tears as David followed Sarah out of the party. Joe made a hard, angry shape as Deb lifted him into her arms.

David was sitting on the stairs, elbows on knees.

'How could you not tell me? I've been begging you like an idiot!' Sarah said.

His head jerked up. 'Sit down, will you. Please.'

She couldn't bear to be still, but he wasn't going to talk to her otherwise. She felt behind her for the hall chair and sat down.

'It wasn't like that.' He chewed on the side of his thumbnail.

'Well, what was it like? David?'

'I hardly remember anything, just a vague thing about waking up to some sort of commotion. Then I must have gone back to sleep. Mum was gone, after that. But it was never talked about.'

Anguish rushed into the stillness Sarah had dreaded; she pictured it coursing through her bloodstream into the baby. 'But Dad must have told you something. Did he tell you not to tell me?'

'No. Well … he just said it was our secret. Then nothing else, ever.' He crouched there, tongue-tied and slow; the scientist with the dry wit quite gone. She had the dangerous sense of violating something that held him together.

'But you kept it from me all these years. Even when I was older. Even after he died.'

'It wasn't like that! I never think about it. It's in the past.'

Heat raged through her. How neat for him – the past all packed up and tidied away! Hers was a freak show; a crime scene. She stood up and the floor wavered; she grabbed at the back of the chair. He clambered from his step and grasped her arm.

'Sarah, be careful. God, what was Uncle John doing, dragging this all up now...'

'Telling me the truth! That's what he was doing!' She shook off his hand with a jab of her elbow. 'Which is more than the rest of you did.'

She turned to the door for a great slamming exit. But balloons and torn wrapping paper littered the floor. Joe's birthday party. How had she not noticed before? She could not even recall seeing Joe or Deb in the other room. All at once it was impossible – nightmarish – that she had stormed in on the wings of such an ugly mood. She remembered the little party they had had when Joe was two.

'Look – say hello to Deb and Joe for me. We're coming over at the weekend, with his present.'

'Sarah...'

'What?'

'Are you all right to drive?'

She nodded, and he moved to open the door for her like a proper host. She stepped over the party mess; the bright remnants of another life.

Joe's head was down as he played with a toy watering can. Deb reached with the flannel, guessing where the dirt was on his face. Sarah had left without speaking to her. Was she upset that Deb had been so busy when she arrived with her terrible revelation? David had told her in muttered bursts after the party guests left, saying 'I don't even bloody remember it'. Cutting his sister's drama down to size. But tears and confrontations were everything he hated.

And here was Joe in his bath; his hair still soft and silky, like a baby's. He had been counting down the sleeps until his party, and it had been ruined. It had taken Deb and Hilary an hour of distracting and cajoling him with his favourite DVD before he had seemed himself again.

A shadow blocked the light and David leaned in the doorway, his eyes unfocused.

'Joe, Daddy's here!' she said, and to him, 'All right?'

'I just don't know why she had to go digging this all up.'

'No... The timing wasn't great. But I suppose it's being pregnant – she's bound to want to know about your mother.'

'But what good does it do anyone?' Joe jolted at the shout, his bottom lip beginning to tremble.

'It's all right, darling!' she said. 'Daddy's not cross with you. Here, he'll give you a big birthday kiss.' She pushed back from the rim of the bath to make room, but David just stared ahead, not seeing Joe's face, tipped up ready for his kiss. He turned and walked away.

The wail began quietly but swelled, echoing off the tiles. Deb closed her eyes for a second. Christ, not again. But no one else was going to deal with it. She dragged herself to her feet. Joe soaked her right through to her underwear as she hoisted him out and wrapped him in a bath towel, a soft weight, sobbing in her arms.

Rebecca pushed into Sarah's office, grasping a printout, and tossed her crinkly hair over her jacket shoulder. She had a habit of challenging half the changes Sarah made to her layouts. Her latest editing job had been sloppily done and had taken Sarah hours to check; arguing over it now would make the book late for its production deadline. Something nagged at the edge of consciousness, but Rebecca was speaking.

'Sarah, I wanted to ask – Oh my God. How grim!'

Sarah's desk was loaded with pictures: medieval lunatics chained in torment; Victorian asylum dwellers undergoing bizarre treatments; people strapped down and wired up for ECT.

'They're for the *Madness* book,' she said. 'I'm sorting them into chapters.' In fact, for some time she had just been staring at them.

'Right. OK... So, for this meeting, are we saying –'

'Meeting?' The printout in Rebecca's hand was not a book layout at all; it was a production schedule.

'The schedules meeting? At ten?' The upward lilt of the phrases said, *Duh?!*

The meeting was at the same time every month, and Sarah always checked the electronic diary first thing. How could she have forgotten? She was supposed to be training Rebecca in just this type of efficiency. She would need a half-hour to prepare, but her monitor showed 9.51 already. She stood up and a pile of pictures slid from her lap on to the floor.

'Oh! Yes – give me a couple of minutes to check something. I'll pop in on my way to the boardroom.' She stooped to grab at the pictures and her bump forced the air from her lungs with a little gasp of strain. These meetings were brisk – she had to be ready to vouch for every stage of all her team's projects. Dates were batted from production to editorial and back at ping-pong speed. Sarah usually found it exhilarating – *yes, I'll be ready with that, I'll turn the ozalids round in a day…* But if anyone wasn't performing well, they were exposed to the judgmental stares of the boardroom.

Rebecca raised her eyebrows and bent to pick up a stray picture: a dead-faced woman with lobotomy scars. She flicked it onto the desk with a flourish. 'It's OK, it's normal to be daffy in your condition.'

CHAPTER FOURTEEN

'David? Are you getting up? Joe's been up for hours.' Deb wrenched the curtain aside with deliberate noise. A rectangle of greyish day surprised the stuffy murk of the bedroom, revealing an overflowing laundry basket and yesterday's clothes on the floor. It was his turn, it had to be.

'Jeezz.' David spoke indistinctly, a hand in front of his eyes.

Deb looked with longing at the limp, crushed form of her pillow. Joe was calling from downstairs. She needed to lie down and be in her own world for a minute, to find – from somewhere – the energy to carry on. But David was squeezing his eyes shut and making an 'mph' noise as though trying to speak. Or – oh God, was he going to be sick?

'Oh! Sorry!' She rushed to close the curtains. David's hand was pressed over his eyes. 'Is it one of your migraines?'

'Mmn.'

He had suffered from severe attacks when she met him, but they had become less and less frequent and then stopped altogether, giving her the pleasant feeling that she had curative powers. There had been bright pink pills, hadn't there, that helped if he took them soon enough? She moved closer and could see even in the dimness his fishy pallor; the grey skin under the eyes. Joe's calls were rising to a continuous shout.

'Should I get you something from the chemist?'

'Mmn.'

'I'll bring you the bucket, just in case. I'm coming, Joe!'

Downstairs, Joe had upended a box of puzzles amid a sea of abandoned toys, and was trying to force a piece into the wrong hole.

'You do it, Mummy!'

'In a minute. We need to get you dressed. We're going to the chemist.'

'No. Not the chemiss.'

In the kitchen, she reached into the cupboard under the sink and rummaged among rags, old sponges and carrier bags. A tin of shoe polish tumbled out and banged her bare toes. She pictured the battles ahead over getting dressed, leaving the house and fastening the car seat. Joe had woken twice in the night; he was probably as exhausted as her. And had she really arranged for the nursery mums and toddlers to come round this afternoon?

David would have to stay in bed – she could see that. As she straightened up with the bucket, though, she remembered the time she had gastric flu, and lay curled round Joe as he watched TV. She had got up at intervals to go and be sick.

Joe stood there, holding out a puzzle piece. 'Mummy's turn.' She could not form the words for a reply.

Mid-afternoon the mums and toddlers from nursery arrived. Joe had crashed out on the sofa, which would be a disaster at bedtime – but she was too exhausted to face him grumpy, so left him to sleep. Halfway through the visit, Hilary turned up.

'Don't ask me about my day,' she said, a shake of her head disturbing the dark curtain of her fringe.

'I need a cuddle from my favourite boy.' She swept past Deb and then saw the other visitors. 'Oh. Hi!' She sat down and made an effort to chat, but she was pale and her smile kept faltering.

She joined Deb in the kitchen at the first opportunity. 'My God, they do go on, don't they?' she said. 'I mean, much as I love Joe, I don't want to know about his every fart!'

'Welcome to my world.'

'It would drive me mad. You'll go back to nursing soon though, won't you?'

'It's not that easy, with the shift work. What would I do about childcare? I don't think David would cope,' Deb said. 'What's up?'

'That big case I couldn't talk about. Well, it doesn't matter now because it's all fallen apart.'

'Oh right. Sorry about that.' Deb didn't have the energy for one of the police sagas with which Hilary held the floor at family get-togethers. She was about to take a tray through to the living room, but Hilary sat down on a kitchen chair.

'It was an abuse case in a school, from years ago. We were going after the headteacher. He's such a bastard, Deb. Not only sadistic, but the most manipulating, aggressive liar. He's got everyone believing he's this pillar of the community, and he's spread lies about his victims that have put everyone off the scent for years. I can't tell you the lives he's ruined. The suicides...'

'God. I had no idea.' Deb's limbs felt full of cotton wool; she could barely push down the plunger of the coffee pot.

'No, well, you don't talk about it. You wallow in some awful shit, but you keep thinking you'll see the victim's faces when they get justice. But the DI called us in this morning. They're dropping the prosecution. They're saying the bastard's got Alzheimer's and isn't fit for trial.'

'Oh Hil. I am sorry.'

'I just want to make an actual bloody difference, you know? I've spent months taking their statements. About the horrible, degrading things that ruined their lives...' Deb handed her a sheet of kitchen paper and she wiped her nose. 'This one guy was gagging, Deb – I mean actually retching when he talked. And there's DI Martin telling us to let it go and move on to the next one. After all that fucking work. I don't think I can do this any more.'

'Oh, love.' Tiredness had made everything surreal: Hilary's crisis and the sound of children playing next door. Deb struggled to think straight as she pulled Hilary close. 'But you love police work, don't you?'

'Not right now, I don't.'

'No but you've always liked being in the know about things most people don't get to hear about. Do you remember you used to make me play detectives?' Deb had found this funny at first, picking someone in town and trailing them – bobbing into doorways when they turned round and scribbling in notebooks afterwards, speculating about what they were up to. But Hilary had been dead serious – she hadn't wanted to give up the chase even if the target got on a bus.

'Funnily enough, it's not quite the same in real life.' Hilary dabbed at her ruined eye make-up. She had always been so proud of her job and could even be dismissive of other people's, as though they could never be as interesting or important.

'But you're good at it. And you care about it. It's just the paperwork and the targets you hate, isn't it? And things like this of course. Didn't a friend of yours leave to work for some agency?'

'Amal. Yeah. He's with this private investigation firm now. But I've never imagined leaving the police.'

'Well, why don't you sound him out? You put your heart and soul into the police. But there's nothing to say you can't use your skills elsewhere. All right?'

'All right.' Hilary sniffed and managed a smile. 'Where's David?'

'In bed with a migraine. He hasn't had one for years.'

'You've had a bad day too.'

Deb nodded, gazing at the floor. It looked absurdly comfortable, a cool place to lay your cheek, but someone was calling from the other room. She put a bright face on and got up to go.

CHAPTER FIFTEEN

27 weeks: By now your baby's eyes will be blue, though later the colour will depend on inherited factors. You may still be feeling energetic, but try not to overdo it. Get as much rest and relaxation as you can.

Brambles and ivy snaked over the brickwork, as though the woods were intent on reclaiming the garden. They looked as abundant as ever to Sarah, who had spent the last hour trying to cut them back and burning the debris. Despite the September chill, she wiped moisture from her forehead with the sleeve of her jumper.

Something shifted beyond the wall. She stopped with her shears poised in mid-air. All she could hear was the sighing of the huge-limbed trees, and a green stem making the bonfire spit and pop. Reaching higher in the mass of poison-green, she chopped again.

Another shuffle. In the bonfire haze, she thought she saw the black wrought-iron ring of the gate turn and the latch lift. The breeze changed direction and smoke wafted over her view. She peered through the billowing cloud – was that a figure in the gateway? Hot vapour veered round and blew, stinging, in her face.

'You'll fight a losing battle against these woods.' A cool draught cleared the air, and Uncle John stood, smiling, between her and the gate. 'Sorry! I didn't mean to startle you. I called at the house but there was no answer. I followed the smoke.'

They sat on the garden bench under ancient, overhanging trees, watching the fire and sipping from their mugs of tea. Sarah had imagined doing this with Jim, but somehow they had never had time. He had driven away an hour ago for another site visit.

'I hope you don't mind me dropping in. I wanted to see how you were, after last time.'

How was she? The landscape inside her head had completely

changed. She and Deb had had no chance to talk. Jim led her away from the subject whenever she brought it up; so she had sunk back inside herself to ponder it alone. 'I'm – OK.'

'Good. Good.' They shared the crackling progress of the bonfire, the embers black and quiet one minute, then fanned into a blaze by the whirling wind. 'A little jumpy, though?'

She turned to see a faint, teasing smile, which surprised her into a laugh. 'I didn't see you come in. You just appeared in the smoke.'

'It's the woods. They've always felt rather creepy here.'

'I'm glad you said that! I thought I was getting a bit irrational!'

'When we were children,' he said, 'I used to tell Mary that demons lived there. I know. Brothers can be terrible.' He gazed into the fire. 'She was terrified of the woods at night. Our father used that once, for one of his experiments.'

A warning chill went through her. 'Experiments?'

'He was interested in twin studies. He'd read articles about some twins having a psychic bond. So every now and then, when this spirit of scientific enquiry took him, he would take one of us aside, and do something to us to provoke a reaction. A member of the clinic staff would observe the other one, to see if they reacted too.'

John saw the flicker of uncertainty in his niece's eyes. Her hands were moulded round her mug; her hair in spirals, escaping from a clip. Mary had told him everything that evening when they were eight, in the cramped darkness of the nursery cupboard. She had still been trembling. The twins had no one else to tell things to. Their mother was always in her room with the door locked, or out somewhere.

Mary couldn't see anything with the blindfold on, but it was soft and springy underfoot, so she guessed they were on the

Woodlands lawn. Father spun her round, which made her laugh at first. He never normally played with them, and certainly never at the clinic. 'Dizzy enough yet?' he said. She said, 'Yes!' She had a sick feeling in her stomach and head. He began to lead her along. She tried to keep smiling, but she almost fell over and he pulled her up by her arm. Mary asked if they were going back to reception and he said, 'That would be telling.'

She was really dizzy now but he took her wrist and pulled her along fast on her wobbly legs. She had no idea which way they were going. They walked on and on and the air had a mushroomy smell. Mary wanted to stop but couldn't say because Father didn't like you complaining. There was crackling under her shoes.

She asked if they were nearly there, keeping her voice jolly.

'One more spin!' He held her arms against her sides and spun her round and round. When he let go, she fell forwards a bit and reached out her hands. She tried to laugh and called out, 'Daddy?' The blindfold hurt her eyes and she felt sick like you do after going on a roundabout. She crouched down, waiting for the spinning feeling to stop, and she could feel sticks and leaves on the ground.

She called 'Daddy!' again.

She stood up and pulled at the blindfold. Her fingernails dug into her skin as it came over her forehead. It was pitch black in the woods and Daddy had gone.

She called, 'Daddy! Daddy!' in case he was hiding behind a tree. But there was no answer. Which way was home in all this blackness? Something swooped at her and flapped in her hair and she screamed and hit out, remembering demons. She started to move forwards blindly and then she saw a tiny light and ran towards it.

John was waiting in the nursery. His toy soldiers were having an irritable, half-hearted battle. A thin, spotty student was watching from a chair. John hadn't been invited when Father took Mary out, and none of his games worked without her. Escape From The

Danger Zone was his latest favourite. The Baron locked them up and they had to get out using Escape Plans from his adventure book. He was the one who knew all the plans – like Escape Plan Fifteen: using wire to make a skeleton key which would work on any lock.

Why wasn't Mary back? The soldier in his hand smashed down on the one next to him and half the battalion spun off and scattered on the floor. The student from the clinic gawped behind his clipboard. Didn't he know it was rude to stare?

There was a noise outside. John went to the window. Leaning his head against the bars, he saw the garden gate swing open. Mary burst from the darkness into the pale light from the house.

'I saw fear on her face beyond all reason,' John told his niece. And God, how his blood beat faster as Mary struggled to breathe through her crying.

'That's terrible. Her own father.' In the fire, a pile of charred wood shifted and collapsed in a shower of whitish ash. As the sticks rearranged themselves, the flames leapt higher. 'Do you think it affected her? I mean, is it why she..?'

'Who can say? She can't tell us now, can she?' He watched firelight dance and flicker, reflected in Sarah's eyes.

The wind had picked up as he made his way homewards; it was threshing through the dried leaves above him. Coming out of the trees on to the Woodlands lawn, he saw the cold strip lighting glaring from the wards and the dirtier glow in the window of the tower. He paused, his breath shaking.

Her hair – her lips parting, plump as a child's, as his story disturbed her – it all played in his head as he trod on the first step of the spiral staircase. His veins sang with her nearness, untainted by the years and returned to him whole, young and alive. Like a sleepwalker, he mounted the tower staircase, barely aware of where he was going and what he was going to do.

He stood at the door and fumbled with the key. What would his staff think if they could see him now – their stern Director, trembling like a schoolboy on a routine visit to a patient? The key turned in the lock and he saw, not the door opening but Sarah turning to look, silk hair straying, eyes all concern, with such a look of her that…

There she sat on the bed, hunched over, her hair wild and unwashed. Sallow skin leathered over her bones and wrinkled around dull, empty eyes. Her mouth hung slack; a string of drool dropping from her purpled lip. He could not bear it – he lurched towards her with the anguish of it raging in his ears.

'Well, my dear! I've been talking about the good old days.' His voice was like venom spitting from his mouth, but it was not relief enough. His arm swung back – he could knock down the tower with the power in his palm – and he slapped her across the face with all his strength.

She gave a cry, but not of surprise. He stood over her, his mouth pooling with saliva. He felt better – not good, but different, as though something had been vented. Her head was turned aside, her nose beginning to bleed. It was ridiculous the way she pulled herself away from him. *Where do you have to go, my darling?* Her hair fell over one side of her face, as if she could hide. He reached out and yanked the tangles aside. Somehow the feel of her skin aroused tenderness – it flooded through his throbbing fingers, sensitised by the slap. She was, after all, completely his.

Still, he must deal with her – and he was about to get a grip on her when he remembered to check the door. *Think, John, damn you.* He pulled back and went to lock it. *Now, give her what she deserves. For losing that trembling beauty. For wanting to get away. Treacherous bitch!* He hauled her nightdress out of the way, unleashed himself expertly and forced his way in, grasping her by the hair and one thin arm. He did not see her for the firelit scene of his fantasy; he was masterful – a new man – and was released, triumphant, in no time.

Afterwards, the perfunctory clean-up with wipes that he carried in his pocket – she hardly bothered for herself these days – and then he manoeuvred the stiff, hunched form into the window chair. He sat down heavily beside her, and reached for her hand. How weak her grip was when he interlaced his fingers with hers, the way he had done since they were children.

'Mary?' Her face was turned away, towards the window. 'Look at me.' Slowly, Mary turned her head. Her nose was still bleeding; he would see to that before he went. There was that desolate look in her eyes. It didn't matter. His earlier unbearable feeling had gone, leaving behind it a peaceful weariness. He felt quite content to sit here and hold her hand; him and Mary, as it had always been. Like a couple locked in marital torment, he thought, with a wry chuckle. A drop of blood fell from her nose on to their entwined hands.

CHAPTER SIXTEEN

Kim's friend, Moira, was on the church welcome team that Sunday, and she pointed Graham out through the crowd having coffee after the service. 'He's been coming for a few weeks and I mentioned he might want to join a house group,' she said. 'I thought you could tell him about yours.'

'Wait, you mentioned it – or he did?'

'I might have planted the idea,' Moira said, with a twinkle in her eye. 'But he didn't look horrified.' She swept away to join another conversation.

Kim peered through the chatting groups and saw a man probably in his forties; his hair still browner than grey. He was scruffily handsome in jeans and a checked shirt, and stood alone, close to the trestle table of coffee percolators and biscuits. People shouldn't cling together in cliques, she thought. The whole point was to show newcomers God's love through the warmth of your welcome – however awkward that felt.

'Hello!' she said. 'I don't think we've met before. I'm Kim. Moira said you might be interested in a house group. It's Graham, isn't it?'

He was looking around him with an assessing, perhaps ironic look that now rested on her. Moira hadn't said if he was completely new to church. How weird it must seem to outsiders – the hands held high during songs, the fervent calling on the Holy Spirit, and then small talk over coffee as though nothing had happened. And now some strange woman harassing him.

'Yes,' he said. 'Hello.'

'I don't know if you're actually interested in a house group,' Kim said. 'I don't want to scare you away.' A smile played round his eyes. He didn't look easily scared.

'I might be,' he said.

'Oh! That's good then. Sorry, I'm not very good at welcoming. We really want people to feel included here, but it's a struggle when you're British, isn't it? We seem to be hard-wired to skirt round anything deep.'

He laughed and sipped at his coffee. 'So tell me about this house group.'

'Well it's at my house, which means no home-made cookies – just a swift hoover round and chocolate Hobnobs. But it's a nice crowd. We have some great discussions – often quite off the subject.' She paused, uncertain now. He might be a long-time churchgoer looking for some stringent Bible study. 'I don't know – are you new to all this?'

'I used to go to church with my wife when my daughter was younger. But it all went by the wayside after the divorce. Or I did.'

'Oh that happens doesn't it? You go a bit off the rails.'

'You're divorced too?'

'Five years ago.' She nodded in the quiet moment that followed. 'How old's your daughter?'

'Fifteen. Going on twenty-five. She keeps trying to get me to go speed dating.'

'Ugh!' Kim said. 'That would be worse than this!'

Then of course she told him about Tom and Amy and the next thing she knew people were drifting off home and Amy had come out of youth group and was standing with her arms crossed, jiggling one leg to show that she wanted to leave. Kim had to scribble down the house group details in a hurry. But it hadn't been awkward after all.

CHAPTER SEVENTEEN

28 weeks: This is the beginning of the third trimester, which is often the most enjoyable part of a pregnancy. You should have plenty of energy to help you prepare for the baby.

Jim chuckled at the radio and turned to share the joke with Sarah, but she was staring ahead. He had got up at the crack of dawn and driven for hours to get home so he could be with her for this antenatal appointment. The car was bumping and churning, struggling to get a grip where days of rain had undermined the woodland path.

'Their own father!' she said. 'For some kind of sick experiment!' He steered between silent black tree trunks. 'What kind of damage would that do to a child?'

'Mmn. How's junior?' he asked. 'Any gymnastics today?'

She gave a tiny shake of her head, perhaps not even in answer to his question. The bottle of organic juice in her hand was open but untouched. He thought of Mum when she got a bee in her bonnet and wouldn't stop worrying, whatever you said. But the comparison jolted him; Sarah was nothing like Mum.

'And what was their mother doing?' The tyres shuddered and slipped and he shifted down into first gear. 'Can you imagine? Jim?'

'No!' he burst out. 'I don't want to, to be honest.'

'Don't want to what?'

'Imagine.' He had got his hopes up that she was getting brighter; she had said on the phone that she'd seen some wallpaper for the nursery, and told him something funny Helen had said at work. But now this.

'Oh well, I'm sorry.'

'No, look. I've just had hardly any sleep. And I wish we could forget all this stuff from your uncle. It gets you so agitated.'

'Well, actually it does. Can't you understand that?'

'No! I can't! I'm trying to, but –'

'But your family's normal. With no awful secrets.'

'It's not that!' he turned sharply towards her, and swung the steering wheel with him. The car lurched to the left and the rear end whirled in a mad half-circle. Time slowed, going who knew where. A tree veered towards their faces as Jim stamped on the brake. They jerked to a halt, back wheels spinning in the mud.

'Shit! 'Jim turned the key, quelling the wailing of the engine. Sarah was bracing herself against the door and the dashboard, red juice dripping from her arms. 'Shit, I'm sorry. I'm sorry.' He had been longing to see her, looking forward to this appointment. 'I'm an arsehole. Sarah? I just don't like you getting upset.'

A damp-blackened tree was only inches from their bumper. A thud shook the car and a huge branch fell from the roof on to the bonnet, followed by a shower of debris. They hunched, arms over heads. When the torrent slowed and stopped, there was a hush as if the woods were waiting for their reaction.

'Are you all right? Sarah?' he cried.

She remained curled over, trembling. 'Can we just go?' He started the engine, struggled into reverse and brought the clutch up slowly. After a moment's wheel-spinning, the car lurched backwards, the fallen branch crashing into the undergrowth. He looked back as if for an assailant, but there was just the bleak path behind them. They bumped round in a quick, ragged arc. He found first gear and the BMW jerked ahead, roaring on its way.

Sarah sat on the examination trolley, looking down at the surgery's threadbare carpet tiles. Tissue paper rustled through her nerve endings every time she moved. The vitamin-and-iron smell of the consulting room met a lingering sick feeling in her gullet. Her new doctor, Ralph Farnham, was young and sporty, with a solid neck and short gingery hair. He was being particularly matey with Jim. The squeeze of the blood pressure cuff relaxed and the gauge shifted and settled. 'Hmm,' he said with a knitted brow.

She rolled down her sleeve and stepped to the floor, joining Jim in the plastic chairs facing the desk. He reached over and took hold of her hand.

'Any family history we should know about?' the doctor asked. 'Your mother's..? Pregnancy and delivery wise..?'

'Oh. No. I mean, I don't know. She died when I was a child.' She sought for something useful to add. 'She had two of us.'

'Oh, that's OK. It's just something we ask. It's not always important.' He continued down her record card. Silly to feel she had let herself down, as though she had missed out a question in an exam. 'Now. Your blood pressure is rather high. That's something we need to keep an eye on in pregnancy.' She knew this, of course; she had read up on everything.

Jim's chair gave a sharp crack as he leaned forwards, releasing her hand. 'Can we do something about that?'

'Well, your wife should make sure she gets plenty of rest...' A flush clashed with the ginger stubble at Doctor Farnham's hairline, and he turned to Sarah with the rest of his answer. 'Keep your intake of salt down to a minimum. I've got a leaflet I can give you. And try to avoid any stress.' She nodded. Of course – she'd do anything. Then she caught Jim's look – as if she were a difficult patient, and needed to be told.

Sarah was trying to reach the car before the moist greyness turned into actual rain, when Jim hooked his arm through hers and held her back.

'What?' Pointedly, she hugged herself against the autumn cold.

'I'm really sorry about before. The car was all over the place and – I worry about you. And with your blood pressure – Sarah, can we try to give it a rest, all this dragging up the past with your uncle?'

'Do you think I went looking for it? Asking for trouble?'

'No but – from now on, if your uncle turns up, can you try to steer him clear of anything upsetting? Maybe tell him you're not supposed to have any stress?'

She saw Uncle John at the fireside, on the verge of his story. Could she cope with any more revelations? 'I suppose. I can try.'

His arms went round her, pulling her head close. His voice vibrated in his chest. 'Promise?'

She shifted her head against him in a pantomime nod. But her mind chased after the missed exam question, the uncle's stories. What lay between blind man's buff, *our own little world* – and the pillow, the tower, the fall?

'I'm going to have a bit of supper,' Jim said. It was evening at the Gatehouse, a couple of weeks later. 'Do you want anything?'

Sarah could not seem to fit in the nutrient-rich hoard she was supposed to eat in a day. Even looking at the glossy pictures of it in her pregnancy book made her turn away, feeling full. But in the evenings she was often hungry for a treat.

'What are you having?'

'Cheese on toast with salad cream.' He licked his lips at her customary disdain.

'Can you get me a bit of cheesecake?' It was her latest guilty favourite, disgraceful with fat and a fruit topping that was really no better than jam. 'It's not for me – the baby wants it.'

Jim laughed, took hold of her chin and kissed her mouth, then went into the kitchen. Soon, football commentary roared from the radio. She caught a waft of cheese toasting and could see him carving her a slice from a frozen disc when her mobile rumbled, lighting up the inside of her bag.

No name came up on the screen, but the voice was unmistakable.

'Yes,' she said when Uncle John announced himself.

'I wondered how you were, after our talk'.

'Oh, I'm trying not to think about it all, to be honest.'

'Well, perhaps that's best.' But it was impossible now not to think of it. Jim was leaning close to the radio, the neck of a beer bottle clasped in one hand. 'I did wonder one thing.'

‘Ah.’

‘Where was your mother? I mean, surely she didn’t let him experiment on her own children like that?’

‘My mother. Mmn, it’s hard to explain. Perhaps I should come and see you.’ Jim was sliding his supper from the grill on to a plate with quick nips of his fingers. The football commentary was rising to a crescendo of expectation. ‘It’s not something I can discuss over the phone.’

She could turn away now, steer him clear of it. But that left her with this scrap of truth, like a half-born thing, raw and exposed. ‘I’ve got a morning off soon, for my scan. Maybe we could meet afterwards.’

‘I should think that would be all right. Yes.’

Jim was looking at her, his head still cocked towards the radio. She rushed through the arrangement and goodbyes.

‘YESSS!’ He went reeling round the kitchen with his beer held aloft. ‘One-nil!’ He came in and presented her with her wedge of cheesecake, wilting at the edges from defrosting too long in the microwave. The hysterical clamour continued behind him. ‘There you go. Who was that on the phone?’

‘Oh, work. Rebecca. She forgot to tell me something and she’s off tomorrow.’

‘Bloody liberty, calling you at home.’ He returned to the kitchen and came back with a plate of oily yellow goo slumped over a slab of toast. As he plonked himself down beside her, she stared at her dessert. Purple jelly trickled down its edges. Her appetite had gone.

CHAPTER EIGHTEEN

The haze, why was it going? Mary was cold where she had been damp and hot before, and the chair arm was hard under her elbow. There was a crushing pain down below. Usually she slipped away from it all – but now she sat and felt it and time went on and on. Pill! That was it, she hadn't had her pill. She sat listening for the nurse, but there were no sounds of life in the tower. And something was welling up; something best lost in the fog. A pill would stop it. But it was spilling over now, and there was no rising above it, no escape.

She burst into the nursery. Bits of twig and leaf clung in her hair. Her dress was stuck to her back. She whirled round, sure that demons had followed her. A screech made her cry out – but it was the cupboard door opening. John was crouching inside. She ran and got in, pulling her heels up – quick! He shut the door and his arm went round her shoulders.

'What's happened? Mary? What's happened?' He interlaced his fingers with hers and she sniffed and shuddered as she told him.

Afterwards, she wiped her nose on her cardigan sleeve. 'I want mummy. Where is she?'

'At another party'.

'I want mummy!'

'You call me a baby if I say that.'

'But it was a really nasty trick!' A fresh, hot burst of tears.

'Mummy's no good for you anyway,' he said. 'She doesn't love you. I'm the only one that cares.' His breath warmed the wetness on her face. He shifted in the cramped space and a tiny strip of light from the crack between the doors showed that he was kneeling. He took her hands and pulled her down onto her knees too. Were they going to say a prayer, like they did at school? Or make a vow – perhaps to look after each other always? Something fluttered at the hem of her dress.

‘Do as I say.’ Her dress was wrenched up. He took hold of the waistband of her knickers and she glimpsed his face looking fierce and hard, the eyes glittering. His fingernails were ragged and sharp, like a demon’s. She had nowhere to run to now.

As Kim opened the door, Jane lurched forwards, her eyes wild. In her throat was a rasping sound like someone trying to cry out from a nightmare.

‘What is it? Jane?’ Kim rushed to crouch at her side and took her hand. A violent trembling coursed between them. At last the rasping came to a stop and Jane breathed in shivery gasps. ‘Are you all right?’ Kim felt the hot, damp residue of panic in the woman’s hand. She rubbed it between her own, and as the nightdress sleeve rode up, she saw a patch of rawness, like a Chinese burn. Self harm? She had been so agitated when Kim walked in, and her face looked blotchy and red. But if she hadn’t done it..? ‘Have you hurt your wrist?’

Jane stared ahead, and then her eyelids drooped and closed. When they opened again, the usual dullness had returned, like a curtain falling. ‘You looked upset, Jane. What was wrong?’ The other nurses thought Kim daft to question her; they talked over the heads of mute patients. But Kim’s heart rebelled at the sight.

The silence lengthened, and she stood up on cramped legs and began to tidy the bed. She must get home. Amy had been quieter than ever since the weekend at Paul’s. Even her phone chats with friends now had a moping and weary tone. Stopping in the hallway last night, Kim had overheard her burst out, ‘It’s nothing. Why can’t people just leave me alone?’ She sighed as she shook out the blanket. There was a tiny sound of something falling to the floor. She would check for it in a minute. ‘I’d love to know what’s on your mind,’ she said. ‘If you could find a way to tell me.’ She turned to see Jane bent forwards, as if she had frozen, caught out in the middle of some secret act. But how silly, of course not.

Kim unhooked the clipboard. There was no tick beside the morning dose of medication. Had the early shift forgotten to tick it, or not come up at all? Jane had had an extra treatment this evening, so had missed that dose as well. Perhaps the sudden withdrawal had caused a panic attack? She was sitting back now, her hands curled tight, her sleeve covering that reddened wrist. Kim picked up a pill tub with a big capsule in it.

'Well, Jane, you seem much calmer now. And this'll give you a peaceful night…' A yawn threatened in her throat. She tipped the pill towards Jane's slack lips, and she accepted it, then turned her head towards the window and fell still. 'You take care,' Kim said, and gave her shoulder a parting squeeze. She might have been talking to a waxwork. Deep in thought, Kim realised halfway down the spiral stairs that she had left the key in the lock, and had to go back up for it.

Dear Uncle John. Mary had been staring at the floor, longing for the mercy of the haze. Then something was wafted towards her by the air from the blanket: a card with neat, flowing handwriting. Something of his – she remembered him taking off his jacket and flinging it down. But then she read in snatches over the nurse's chatter: ... *settled in at the Gatehouse... Sorry to bother you... key to the attic?...* Sarah. She leaned down, quick as a thief, while the nurse was over by the bed.

Now footsteps descended the stairs. Alone, Mary uncurled her fist and the card sprang open.

SARAH AND JIM MERCER HAVE MOVED TO: THE GATEHOUSE, WOODLANDS ESTATE, NR. ASHBURY, KENT.

Her fingers closed around it again, but gently, as though it were a fragile creature. She raised the other hand to her lips, and spat out the gelatine capsule. It lay on her palm, glistening, whole. Mary looked at the window, towards the woods and beyond. She saw her face, staring, ghost-like in the darkened glass. It said that everything had changed.

CHAPTER NINETEEN

32 weeks: Your baby is now perfectly formed, and his proportions are much as you would expect them to be at birth. It is important that you learn to relax both physically and mentally in preparation for the delivery.

'I'll tell David on you!' Sarah whispered as the sonographer's gelled instrument slipped across her bump. Jim was blinking away a liquid sheen brimming in his eyes.

'I've got something in me eye,' he said, staring at the screen. The baby had a face and hands, a tiny pumping heart and shining white bones. It lay, curled and floating, in a dark water world inside her.

They emerged from the hospital into the glow of a late October day, each holding a corner of the photograph. From the black and white jumble of pixels, you could pick out the over-sized head; the swollen eyelids; the little face in profile. They tussled and tripped, and clutched at each other, laughing.

'I'd better get going,' Jim said. 'I've got that meeting. Are you going straight to the office?'

For a moment she thought she was, with this heady elation to buoy her into work. But then she remembered. 'I think I'll have a walk through the park first. Get some fresh air.' 'OK. I'll see you tonight, then. Look after that kid.' The look on his face as he kissed her lingered in her mind as she watched him walk away.

It was one of those rare autumn days of misty distances and golden light. She and Uncle John had arranged to meet in the park café next to the hospital. She began to walk along the path, looking at mothers and children heading for the play area. Her talks with her uncle played back to her: in the attic, the woods and the garden. All that time, this little being had been growing, feeding from her, trusting her, depending on her for life. She had a moment's lurching vertigo and slowed her pace, fingernails denting the insides of her fists.

When she looked up, he was standing in her path in his dark overcoat, watching some little girls on the swings. Sarah picked up her stride and went towards him, holding the scan photograph in front of her.

'Hello,' he said. 'Are you well?'

'Yes, thank you. Really well. Look! I've just had it done.'

He looked at the picture as though he didn't quite know what to make of it. 'Yes, I see. Well, shall we..?'

She had shown a man she hardly knew a picture of her womb. She stifled laughter – Jim would fall about when she told him later. But no – of course, he couldn't know.

The café was in an airy conservatory, with light slanting through potted trees onto the tables. A mother sat at the next table with a baby standing on sturdy little legs on her lap. He looked over his mother's shoulder at Sarah, who spent delighted moments making him smile.

'I just feel that this is my chance to put everything right,' she said, clasping her thick white teacup when their drinks arrived. 'I was so upset by what you told me, and you've been a great help, but I've got to put it all behind me and move on.'

He sighed and pushed a hand through the thin hair on the top of his head.

'What?' she said.

'One would hope that you can … put everything right … put it all behind you. You don't even know the whole story.'

She could take her photograph and leave now – escaping into the bright world above. But some cursed thing made her ask. 'You mean about my mother?'

'You asked about my mother,' he said. The baby at the next table made a playful grab for Sarah's hair. His mother soothed and chuckled in the background as Uncle John went on. 'She was what you might call a party animal. Always going out somewhere that sounded fun. We'd lie in our beds, listening to her getting ready. There'd be loud voices, her laughing… doors slamming. There was a kind of sociable frenzy about her then. But the end was … very different.' Something nagged at Sarah's edges, something huge and looming. The baby's fat little fist swooped again, after a curl. 'Then one day she was gone and no one told us why. I went to the clinic to look for my father and I heard the staff gossiping. *There's no question,* one said. *It was Mrs Briers!* They'd heard a rhythmic thumping in one of the padded cells. They ran in to find her having a fit. She was in a straitjacket, and she had choked. It was too late to save her. The cell was so bare, there wasn't even a sheet to pull over her face. They said how terrible she looked. How beautiful she had been before.' He shook his head. 'You asked why she didn't protect us from our father. Well that's why. She was losing her mind.'

'But – why? I mean, what was wrong with her?'

'Her illness began when she had us. Just as Mary's did when she had your brother.'

Sarah's cup clacked in her saucer and the baby at the next table jolted, his joyful expression falling.

'Wait – is that why you've told me? Because I'm pregnant? Are you saying it's in the family?'

'There's no proof of that. It was only ever speculation. Sarah? If you're forewarned...'

'I should get back to work.' Her chair screeched on the floor tiles. Everyone in the café turned to look. The baby began to cry and his mother pulled him close and turned quickly away.

The tiled floor of the conservatory gave way to the tarmac outside. Footsteps were following her.

'Sarah!' Her uncle reached her side, holding out the scan photograph.

She stared at the *32 wks* printed in the corner. 'Why didn't you tell me before?'

'Sarah, let me help you. I'm here to help you.'

The path was shifting beneath her. He put a hand on her elbow. It seemed to hold back the crisis she had felt coming. If he let go, she might slip to the ground.

Jim was hurtling about the nursery trying to get everything finished when Deb and David arrived. The room looked more promising than when Deb had last seen it: yellow paper hid the blighted surface of the walls.

'It's just the teddy bear border now,' Jim said. 'Can you help me match up the ends? Then we'll get it all tidy before Sarah gets home.'

Joe had fallen asleep in the car on the way over and now drooped on Deb's hip.

'So how was the scan?' she asked as Jim climbed on a chair.

'Fantastic! Sarah was thrilled. We were laughing like kids. We couldn't stop smiling.'

'That's brilliant!' When they had last met, Deb had tried to talk about getting ready for the baby, but Sarah had kept drifting away to some dark place within herself. 'I'm so glad. Babies heal things, you know.' David snorted from up his stepladder. 'It's true!' she said. Joe had been their new beginning, come to right the wrongs of her parents divorcing, of David losing his.

'That's it, isn't it?' Jim called, standing on a chair. 'Is it, Dave?'

'God, I don't know.'

'Well, look at the feet – and the paws, and the bow, and the fluffy ear! Are they all matching up?'

'Feet, paws, bloody bow, sodding fluffy bits – yes!'

Joe was getting too heavy to hold like this – Deb would feel the ache in her bones tomorrow, but she hugged him close.

'You said you had news as well?' said Jim, clomping back down to floor level.

'I've been looking at nursing jobs,' said Deb. ' I've always ended up thinking I'd never fit the shifts in with Joe's routines. Then I saw this ad, for manager of CareCorps Nursing Agency. It's local and office hours.'

'So you went for it..?'

'Yes and they seemed to like me at the interview, as if I was a proper person with skills or something. Anyway, I heard today, I've got it!'

'Fantastic!' said Jim. 'Well done, Deb! We'll make this a double celebration.'

'I can't wait to tell Sarah.' There were things only Sarah knew about Deb. Only she would understand the excitement after feeling so buried in motherhood, the trepidation about actually making it work. A complex system of arrangements involving Mum and David had been organised, which all parties had agreed to, apart from the heavy little person in her arms.

A car sounded on the gravel outside. David came down the ladder and there was slapstick cursing and stage whispering as they rushed to tidy away the evidence of decorating. Jim sprinted into the next room and came back grasping the stems of four glasses and, in the other hand, a bottle of champagne, sloshing around in the hurry.

'That's going to be a bit lively, isn't it, Jim? You haven't won a Grand Prix!'

'Yeah and don't get champagne all over my teddy bear border,' David said. 'I've just got the fluffy bits to match!'

They took their places, each holding a full glass. Slow, heavy footsteps came up the stairs.

'Shhh!' Deb whispered into Joe's soft neck. 'It's a big surprise for Auntie Sarah. Wait till you see her face!'

'I'm in the nursery!' Jim called, and they held their breath as the footsteps stopped outside. The door was pushed open. Sarah appeared, her hair in disarray, her eyes lilac-rimmed.

'Surprise!' They raised their glasses. Sarah's gaze went to the walls of the nursery, then up to the teddy bear border.

'Double celebration!' Jim called out. 'First, for baby Mercer, whose nursery I officially declare ...' The power was draining from his voice. 'Open.'

'Oh! Thank you!' But Sarah's face contorted and tears began as she turned to look at Jim.

CHAPTER TWENTY

33 weeks: You may be aware of your baby getting hiccups when he swallows amniotic fluid. Make sure you have the baby equipment you need. It is time to begin preparing for family life.

'Hey, fat girl.'

Sarah did not look up. She had had the dream again last night. It started with a woman's soft hair brushing her face. She smelled warm skin, face powder – every earthly comfort. She reached out for it, but then saw a figure fleeing down an endless white corridor. She ran after her, but she was always too far behind; she tried to call out, but her voice had no power. Her mother ran round a corner without looking back. Dragging sleep-heavy legs, Sarah came to the turning – but found cold air, white light, wind howling in a void.

The aura of it had clung to her all day. She sat now at the computer in a pool of evening lamplight. Something good. Wasn't that the dream's conviction – if she could only reach the fleeing figure? A kiss prickled her cheek, and Jim's words broke through to her at last. She forced a tiny smile. What if her mind had locked out good memories as well as bad?

'What's this?' Jim was sifting through the printouts on the desk. *Mental Illness – a Hereditary Factor?; Post-partum psychosis; Genetic Counselling in Pregnancy; Depression and Heredity.*

'Don't muddle them up,' she said. One pile was more frightening and one more optimistic; the rest of the articles were spread out in no-man's land in between.

She picked up a paper to talk him through it, but as she opened her mouth, there was a soft little thump inside her. She should take Jim's hand so he could feel the baby moving, but the notion foundered and sank. 'It says here that depression and schizophrenia can be hereditary.' Out of her own mouth, she had condemned herself.

'The doctor told you not to worry.' His hand closed around hers.

I'm not your Mum, worrying about nothing, she wanted to say. *You can't just soothe this away.* 'He's not an expert in mental health. All he wants to talk about is my blood pressure.'

He gazed at the pregnancy book on the arm of the sofa. The 33 weeks spread showed the equipment they were supposed to be buying for the baby.

'Blimey. Where are we going to put all this lot?'

What had Pat been like when Jim was a child? She had once had to take to her bed 'with her nerves', she had told Sarah, and they had kept him away from her for weeks. When he was allowed back, she said, her loving little toddler had a tough guy's sticking out chin. Was that how it had been with Mary? Had she always been ill when her children were little?

'I always wondered why I didn't remember being a little girl.'

He let go of her hand.

Kim stepped into the murky light of the tower room. 'I haven't come to be your nurse tonight, Jane.' Hunched in her window chair, Jane moved her head only a fraction; the night sky a black frame around her. Silence rang in the sour air. Kim tipped up a bag and a bright jumble fell onto the bed: a hairbrush, bottles of fruit-coloured gloop, a travel hairdryer, long-bladed scissors and a fluffy towel. 'I'm going to be your hairdresser.'

She stepped over to Jane and placed a gentle hand on either side of her head. There was a waft of unwashed scalp; the hair beneath her fingers frizzing out or clumped in hanks.

'There's nothing to perk you up like a new hairdo. First I'll give it a lovely wash.' She helped Jane up and she stood unmoving while Kim filled the tiny, cracked basin. With firm but gentle pressure, Kim cajoled the stiff back into bending. She had to refill, shampoo and rinse again and again. 'My Mum used to wash our hair at the kitchen sink,' she said. 'My sister used to cry, but I always loved it.' She hummed, recalling the reverie brought on by the warm water, the caressing movement of her mother's hands.

Jane's expression was as vacant as ever. Was Kim mad, trying to make a difference in this intractable gloom? Was she even disturbing her patient? But when Jane was settled back in the window chair and Kim stood behind her with the hairdryer and brush, the strangest transformation took place: the room became a salon, and she relaxed into the chatter of a stylist.

'I'm off home after this – see if I can get a word or two out of my teenagers. I'm quite worried actually, about Amy. She seems very down. I'm even thinking of ringing her father. He remarried a few years ago.' Perhaps it was the warmth of the hairdryer, the soporific motion of the brush, but Jane seemed to have lost some of her stiffness, and her neck gave a little with each gentle pull. Kim moved round her, taking long grey strands from her forehead on to the brush. They were drying smooth and springy, with even a hint of shine. 'I'd have to swallow my pride though; I like him to think I'm doing a great job of bringing them up without him! Well, I'm sure you can imagine. Have you been married?'

Jane looked for a split second right into her eyes. Kim's brush stopped, poised in mid-stroke. But then the pale gaze slid away, and after a moment, she continued with her styling. 'It's not that I'm still angry. I mean, I was, of course – well, he left me for her – for Julie. I prayed to feel forgiving. But I was just furious and bitter.' She moved between Jane and the window. Words she had never intended flowed on the warm air; and half of Jane's head was renewed, like a dead thing brought back to life. 'I told anyone who'd listen what they'd done to us, on and on like a broken record. Then one day I prayed with this lady at our church, and I started to feel I was moving on.'

She tailed off, the tightness in her throat surprising her after all this time.

'Well, to cut a long story short, Julie had some problems of her own and that was a turning point. I should ring, really. See if they can shed any light on things. There. I think you're done!'

She had forgotten to bring a mirror, but the window and the background night did almost as well. She crouched beside Jane and they looked at her reflection. Her hair looked fuller and longer. Its smooth frame revealed a good bone structure, strong eyebrows and lips and china-blue eyes. Kim put a hand over hers. 'You look beautiful. Thank you for listening. And if you ever want to talk, I'm here.' She thought she saw the eyes look out of the darkness, directly into hers. But it wasn't a real mirror and she couldn't be sure.

Silent for decades, Briers had said. Was there nothing to say? Or did the silence hold back unspeakable things? Kim ached to know as she drove the wooded path homewards.

Jim turned the corner into the road in which he grew up. Its boxy houses, all pebble-dashed by the council in the 1950s, had been made more individual by the occupants since: one brightly painted and hung with baskets of winter pansies; another cracked and mossed over, with a boarded-up window and a sofa outside, bleeding stuffing. Jim scanned as usual for estate agents' signs, but then found himself staring at the pink-slabbed pavements, where he had juddered over bumps on his boyhood bike, and later slid home from a teenage pub crawl one icy Christmas Eve, heady with beer and anticipation.

He stopped in front of the house with its tiny square of lawn, and through the glass, the lace curtains Mum was forever washing. Dad's elderly Fiesta, kept roadworthy by his son-in-law, George, took up most of the concrete drive. Jim parked the BMW with a glance around him: there were people round here who would key the paintwork. But George always asked after it as though it were a relative. He had been looking forward to the distraction of laughter and effortless food. 'I'm going to feed that girl up,' Mum had said. 'She's got so thin.' But Sarah was too tired and couldn't face it. As his lips searched hers that morning, he saw in close-up the sharp angle of her jaw and collarbones and the hollows around her eyes. 'Brace yourself,' he said. 'Mum'll cook double and send you a food parcel.' Sarah rolled her eyes as she shut the door.

He cut the velvet purr of the engine. As he stepped into the chill air, the aroma of hot fat and gravy seeped from the house, stirring a hunger he hadn't realised was there.

'Hello!' Dad gestured with a grimace towards the kitchen.

Mum, in mid-flow, was bending over the oven in a cloud of steam: '...all right for you, you haven't got to deal with it...'

'Jim's here!'

'Oh!' Mum straightened up. 'Why didn't you -? Oh, now I'm all...' The oven door banged shut, and Jim's sister Sharon's children appeared in the hallway: seven-year-old Layla in a dress of pink satin and netting, and toddler Dan, wearing only a miniature West Ham shirt and one sock. The two small faces swivelled towards their Nan. Pat plonked a tea towel down and came over, looking steamed. 'Hello, duck. Come on in. I don't know what it'll be like, I don't know if I'm coming or going today. Your father got the wrong gravy granules and says no one will notice.'

'The wrong gravy? That's it, I'm getting right back in the car and going home.' Jim stuck his head round the door of the living room and said hello to the crowd: George standing in front of the gas fire cradling a beer; Sharon on her knees by an empty changing mat, a nappy in her hand, and Auntie June holding a plastic tiara and a glass of sherry.

He followed Mum to the kitchen. 'Bloody hell, it's hot in here, Mum. Shall I open the back door?'

'No! I'm keeping the heat in for the Yorkshires. So. No Sarah then?'

'No, like I said, she needs to catch up on some sleep. The baby's been keeping her awake.'

'Really? Is that it? Only, she's got so thin, Jim.'

'She's always been slim. It helps with my fantasy of being married to a supermodel.'

'But what about the blood pressure? She's not getting that enclampsia thing is she?'

'No of course not. They're just keeping an eye on it. She's fine.'

'Oh, because I – I do worry. You would tell me, wouldn't you, if there was anything?'

'Mum, it's fine.' Jim leaned his back against the work surface, heat prickling the roots of his hair.

'Oh. That's all right then.' She rattled frozen peas into a saucepan and stirred the gravy.

'Give the man a bleedin' break, Pat. He says she's all right.' Dad was in the doorway, waving aside the steam.

'Oh, you can keep out of it. Beef gravy, Jim, with chicken. The one thing he had to do. As if I haven't got enough on my mind.'

'Come on Jim. I'll get you a drink. Before she calls the gravy police.'

'Bloody common sense police, more like.'

There were things Jim had put aside to tell Mum, cheering, funny things – but they seemed to have slipped from his mind, so he followed Dad out. In the living room, Sharon grabbed Dan by the waistband of the tiny jeans he was only half in, and hoiked upwards so that he was shunted into them by gravity. George and Jim talked football and the BMW, and Sharon caught Jim's eye and mouthed, 'Sarah all right?' Jim was giving her a qualified nod, when Auntie June burst into the conversational muddle she couldn't hear:

'I thought we were going to see Sarah. Is she all right?'

The chatter faltered and Jim had to reply into a sudden silence.

'Yeah, the baby's keeping her awake at night but – she'll be fine.' The talk was slow to get started again. It was a relief when Mum called that the roast was ready.

They crowded round the table that almost entirely filled the dining room. 'Help yourselves. I don't know what it'll be like. Have plenty. Can I send some back with you for Sarah, Jim? Would she like that? Will she eat it?'

'Yeah, she'll love it.'

'Well, I hope so. She's so thin, Sharon. These tiny arms and legs and this big bump. The baby's all right though, is it? Because you do wonder, don't you, if the mother's not right...'

Jim looked down at the food she had piled in front of him; enough to feed the labourer he no longer was. The chicken was dry at the edges and the gravy had a salty, artificial smell. Perhaps he should have stayed at the Gatehouse with Sarah? But he saw now, in the angle of her head as he kissed her goodbye, her impatience for him to leave. A tightness pressed at his throat, but Mum was looking over and he loaded his fork with chunks. Imagine the fuss if she thought he had lost his appetite too. 'It's all fine,' he said, and bit down hard.

Amy came into the kitchen, ending a call on her phone. 'Why doesn't Tom have to do it? Why's it always me?'

'He's doing the washing up later. And I fancied your company.'

Amy began to pull the outer leaves off a cabbage. 'Can I eat in my room?'

'No! It's a Sunday roast! We'll eat together, like a family.' When Paul first left, sitting up at mealtimes with the fourth side of the table empty had felt wrong, like eating in a play. But when they lapsed into meals in front of the TV, conversation had died too.

Kim shook the hot pan of roast potatoes. 'Who was that on the phone?'

'Natasha.'

'Oh. How is she? Has she stopped that ridiculous diet?'

'She's not being ridiculous!'

'Oh. You said she was just eating apples…'

'Well, she's under a lot of stress. She was going out the other day and her Dad was all, "Those jeans are a bit tight, aren't they? Why didn't you get a bigger size?"'

'Oh for goodness sake! Men can be so insensitive, can't they? Although I don't think Dad would say anything like that to you.'

Amy seemed to be stabbing the cabbage with the paring knife instead of slicing it. 'He can be insensitive too.' Her voice had gone tight.

Letting the oven door swing shut on the roasting pan, Kim looked up to see fat tears dropping on to the cabbage. 'What is it, Amy? What is it?'

Amy's voice rose almost to a squeak. 'I asked him about the

holiday...' Paul and Julie were taking Amy to Thailand – not Tom because he had mock exams. Amy had bought a bikini and told all her friends. 'He said he wasn't sure about it any more, we'd have to see. And when I got upset, he said, "It's not all about you, Amy". Like I was some spoilt brat.' Her shoulders were shaking and snot fell from her nose.

'Oh darling. You must have felt awful.'

'I didn't want to go round there again but I made myself, I thought he might say he was sorry but – he was all quiet and off with me. If it was just money or something, he'd say, wouldn't he? It must be that they don't want to take me... I feel so shit, Mum. I don't know what to do.' Kim wrapped her daughter in her arms. When her sobbing at last subsided, she handed her a wad of kitchen paper.

'I understand how you feel, love. And I could shout in your bloody father's face. But you know, he does love you. He would never want to hurt you.'

'Well he has.'

'Yes. It's like we were saying, men can be dense. I'll give him a call later and see what's going on. But let's get a nice fat roast inside us first. I'm just going to peel off these snotty cabbage leaves and you can chop up the rest. We won't tell Tom.'

Amy took a shuddering breath and smiled for the first time in weeks.

'I just said the holiday would have to wait,' Paul said when Kim called that evening. 'I didn't mean to hurt her feelings.'

'I'm sure you didn't. But she's been thinking all sorts.'

'It's just the situation has changed at the moment, hopefully in the future...'

'Paul, a girl of Amy's age needs her Dad to think she's the best thing ever.'

'I do think that!' He sounded harassed.

'Well, good. But you need to show her. So she can feel it.'

There was a whoosh of static on the line. 'I'll make it up to her. Maybe I'll take her out on her own. Spend some time with her.'

'Yes, that would be good. Thank you. And let's keep in touch. About – how she is.'

'OK. Yes.'

Hanging up, Kim was shaken by two great, dry sobs, and didn't even know who they were for. She had said her piece for Amy, and she had stayed calm. She went to get herself a glass of wine.

She had taken up her usual post on one end of the sofa, an evening of television stretching in front of her, when Tom put his head round the door. 'Have you seen my controller?'

She shook her head and he rummaged under a cushion, grabbed the contraption and turned to go. He had school in the morning, but she called out after him, 'I'm going to watch some really unsuitable rubbish on the telly. Do you want to join me?'

CHAPTER TWENTY-ONE

34 weeks: Your baby's skin is becoming pinker, and she can tell the difference between light and dark. Start to make plans for the early days of motherhood. Organise for your Mum or someone you trust to come and help you.

'What if there are good memories I'm missing out on too?' Uncle John had appeared on Sarah's doorstep half an hour after Jim left. They sat facing the mantelpiece, where Stargazer lilies dropped clumps of rusty pollen. She had clicked on the heating as she ushered him in, and the warming air filled with the mournful scent of the flowers. 'I have this sense that there are good things, if only I could reach them.' He was dressed for work, in a dark-grey jacket, even on a Sunday. He didn't reply. 'It's so stupid and irrational, going round in my head. I can't explain it to anyone.'

'Not even Jim?'

She shook her head, picturing him now amid the rowdy jollity of his family, and felt a disloyal stab of annoyance. 'He'd think I was making things worse.'

'Yet it seems reasonable to me that you're curious.'

'Does it?'

'Of course. There's an important part of your history that you can't remember for yourself.'

'That's it exactly.' An ache in her shoulders seemed to fall away. 'I've got nothing to go on except the things people have told me. But they're just fragments. It's like trying to get a foothold on a pile of rubble.' The word crumpled in her throat.

'Sarah, I'm here to help. Memories are in my line of work, you know.'

'Your work?' she said. 'You mean you think I need a psychiatrist?'

'That's not what I meant. I'm not a psychiatrist anyway, just a doctor. But when I took the clinic over from my father, I knew that we needed to keep up with the times. Nowadays we offer alternative therapies. I wonder – have you heard of hypnotherapy?'

'I know someone who had it to give up smoking,' she said. 'But I don't know much about it.'

'You have to forget the end of the pier show stuff, the stage hypnotists. It is quite an accepted tool among therapists now. It can be very effective in releasing buried memories. We could try it, if you like.'

They might have been talking about changing her hairstyle. 'What if I remembered something bad?' she said.

'That's not in the nature of hypnotherapy. The therapist uses only positive words to speak into the unconscious. That's why it is used to combat stress. It feeds calming, helpful thoughts into the control centre of the mind.'

'Really?'

'Sarah, in my work I've seen adults thrashing and weeping like helpless children, over traumas that are decades old. But a few well-chosen images can help to cast them out. And, as you have said, who knows what good things might be uncovered?'

He stood up. 'We could at least go somewhere with the right associations.' She hesitated, leaving him standing with the smile stiffening on his face. She leaned forwards and he took her hand. His felt slightly damp and swollen like an over-ripe fruit. His arm went rigid, pulling against her weight, and she tottered to her feet with an apologetic puff. He moved off towards the stairs and she went with him.

She couldn't lie on her back these days; the weight of the baby pressed the air out of her lungs. She settled on her side on the nursery sofa. Uncle John had pulled up the wicker chair, with cushions that matched the curtains. He was speaking close to her ear.

'You are in a beautiful garden. You are calm. You are peaceful.' His voice led her in reassuring waves, even as tiredness hauled her down. Perhaps she should apologise now in case she fell asleep? But she couldn't find the strength to interrupt.

'You come to some steps. You go down the first one, and every part of your body relaxes. You are filled with peace. Now you go down the second step. Your mind and body relax even more. With every step, you feel more peaceful...'

She followed him downwards through the flowers he suggested, the sunlight filtering through leaves, the trickling of a stream. *I'm going to be very hard to hypnotise*, she thought. *I always want to be in control.* But with each descent came a gentle unravelling within. *I'm such a sceptic, though; I always have been. I take after Dad.*

'You feel totally safe as you listen to my voice. At the bottom of the steps, you will let everything else go from inside your head...'

Imagine – a cloud of toxic darkness expelled from her, dispersing over the garden. 'Nine, ten. The garden is fading away. You are here at the Gatehouse. As you look at the nursery around you, you begin to move backwards through the years.' *That's quite corny. And unlikely.* She opened her eyes by mistake and stared at a teddy bear on the wall. You couldn't be hypnotised with your eyes open, but tiredness and peace had made dead weights of her limbs. Could she even move if she wanted to? Normal life was suspended in the stillness. She could hear Uncle John breathing. His voice was quiet, but very close. 'You are going to remember something that happened here when you were a child.'

The yellow wallpaper with the teddies peeled away in one sheet, like a calendar page in an old film, showing the passing of time. Underneath was the old brown paper, with faded flowers. As she watched, the brown went darker, and the flowers glowed bright as new. 'Something very bad,' said Uncle John.

'Come on, snuggle up with me and we'll have a snooze,' Mummy said, and Sarah rolled into the warm dip beside her in the middle of the double bed.

When she woke up, Mummy had gone. Sarah padded down the hall. Her hand turned the shiny white handle of the nursery door.

Perhaps David was home from school. His pyjamas were where he had dropped them on the orange carpet, over his shoebox of cars, but he wasn't there. She turned to go.

A screech made her jump and she stared at the creepy old cupboard, which looked like the big house where mad people lived. Sometimes, in bed at night, she imagined them lurking inside it, trying to get out. Once she made David check, but he laughed at her. The cupboard made the noise again.

'David?' she said loudly, to scare the night-time things away. The cupboard door was opening. She wanted to run, but she couldn't move.

Uncle John was sitting with his legs up inside. He smiled and put a hand to his lips. Sarah tried to smile back but her face wouldn't move. He pointed a finger at her and then curled it up to say *come here*. It seemed rude not to go to him. His grin stretched wider and he reached out. Dark hairs peeped from under his shirt sleeve.

'Come on in. It'll be our special hiding place. Our secret!' Sarah clasped her hands and twisted, her head on one side, as if she could wriggle away. Uncle John's voice was sharp and jolly; like grown-ups just before they get cross. 'Sarah!' he said. 'Come on!'

'You are back in the garden, walking up the steps. With every step, you feel a bit more awake. When you reach the top, you will not remember my words, but you will remember what you have experienced. Ten... nine...'

She felt incredibly relaxed, but couldn't help being disappointed; she hadn't retrieved any memories at all. 'Five... four... three...' She was still muffled by a great blanket of calm. 'Two... one. Sarah?'

A teddy bear was juggling orange balls on the nursery wall. At the sound of her name, she found she could turn her head after all. Uncle John's pupils were big and black, and his lower lip was shining. There were specks of grey hair in the pores of his face. Her mind struggled to surface, as if from sleep.

'Come back now, Sarah. You are here. What you have seen is all in the past.'

She seemed to make another surge upwards. Had she, after all, been on some other level within herself? She managed to bend her knees and get her feet to the floor.

'Here,' he said, and took hold of her hands. His touch went through her like a current. He hauled her into a sitting position and smiled. Why were her nerves screaming, telling her to run?

'These things can be very powerful, Sarah. We need to take care of you.' His arms went round her and he patted her on the back. The baby squirmed in her womb, compressed by his embrace. His stubble was snagging in her hair. She saw the old nursery cupboard over his shoulder; its door gaping open – and in a rush, she remembered.

CHAPTER TWENTY-TWO

Without the pills, the hours dragged in the creaking darkness and thoughts rose and swelled from the depths, threatening to break their banks and flood.

'Do you fancy a drink?' said Mr Greaves.

Mary was helping out at the village school. He was their newest teacher, just qualified. Dark sideburns framed his boyish face. She looked up from tidying the library shelf and he was pulling a denim jacket over his teacher's shirt and tie.

'Are you coming, Miss Briers?' called the secretary, who usually gave Mary a lift home in her Hillman Imp.

'I'm just doing some tidying for Mr Greaves.'

'Suit yourself!'

'Michael,' he said, as the smart heels clacked away. What sort of girl did she look like, turning down her lift? 'Sorry, he said. 'Have you got other plans? A boyfriend..?'

'Just cooking my father's tea. He says I can keep house for him, since I failed my exams.'

'You can always retake,' he said. 'You'd make a great teacher. You're so good with the children. Lively and animated. And you've got a special touch with the shy ones and the troubled ones. As if you understand them.' Lively and animated? Dull and awkward, more like. Especially with men. John said they wanted her for only one thing. John wasn't here though, was he? 'Does your father insist on an early tea?'

'No. He's always late back from the clinic. I end up eating on my own.'

'We could pop to the White Hart, then. What do you think?'

Their evenings in the pub became a fixture. Michael told her that she was good at things and that she was beautiful. When her heart raced, she thought it must be love, though sometimes it felt like hurtling towards something and not knowing how to stop.

Mary sat under the low beams of the village hotel, amid the glint of glass and silver, and her face ached from smiling for the staring wedding guests. She had been looked at all day long; now more than ever as her father stood up to make his speech.

'As many of you know, I am a man of science, not much given to fancy words. But somehow, while I have been occupied about my business, Mary has found herself a husband. And well, women these days seem to get what they want, don't they? So Mary has got Michael, and it's my duty, so I'm told, to raise a toast to the bride and groom.' Some of the watching smiles had gone rigid, and hands paused, not sure whether to go for applause. A sound cut the air like a slap. Mary turned to see John with his hands together, his gaze fixed on the floor. But then everyone else clapped too and Michael put his arm around her.

'And I've got what I want. I've got you.'

She looked out over her sparkling wine. John's hair had grown longer at medical school and his face looked unusually white. He had not met Michael until today. It must be strange for him, coming home to find her in this whole new world. He drained his glass and his stare pierced her and swept past, discarding her. There was a falling, loosening feeling in her gut.

'Are you going to change?'

She couldn't think what Michael meant, but then remembered her going away outfit waiting in a room upstairs. She pulled back her chair and gathered the springy skirt of her dress in both hands. Gazes followed her as she made her way across the room, her high heels wobbling in the soft pile of the carpet.

She climbed wine-red stairs, through a dimness cast by dark wooden panelling. On the landing she saw her reflection in a long mirror, speckled with rust, and stood for a moment gliding her hands over the silk of her dress. Its pearl shine gave a glow to her skin, pointing out the blue of her eyes. She heard the door of the reception room open, releasing a clamour of voices, then close. Was Michael following her? She needed a moment alone.

The room was creaky and panelled like the hallway, and her outfit was laid out on the bed: a short orange dress with a white belt and collar, and a white patent-leather handbag. It looked shockingly modern in the Tudor setting of the bedroom. New clothes for a new Mary: Mary Greaves. She had retaken her exams and would be looking at teacher training colleges if she passed, which Michael said she was sure to. She had a picture of them in years to come, heading home together at the end of the school day. She reached a hand up over her shoulder, feeling for the catch at the top of her dress.

The door flew open like an explosion and banged abruptly shut. She whirled to find John turning the key. She saw his black-eyed pallor and then his hands made searing pains, grasping the skin of her arms. She was on her back, the air knocked out of her, crushing her new outfit on the bed. His face was distorted and his knee ground into her thigh, trapping her beneath his weight. He tore at her garter with its 'something blue' forget-me-knot; and at her satin French knickers, bought for tonight. He gouged his way in and rammed a furious rhythm through flesh and muscle and bone.

'For letting that bastard get his filthy hands on you.' His head knocked her temple; his face hot and livid. 'They think you're a pure little bride. But I know you. I've always known you. This is what you are.'

He gripped her hips through handfuls of her wedding dress, and as he heaved at her in one final lunge, the bodice ripped away from the skirt, and she knew it was ruined.

CHAPTER TWENTY-THREE

A smart woman caught Deb's eye in the hall mirror. Her suit, bought to celebrate her last promotion, was a classy, just-shimmering blue. Joe bowled into her legs with all the force in his three-year-old frame.

'Mummy's got to go now,' she said. 'Daddy's taking you to play school today.' David shuffled out of the kitchen, head down. 'I'm off then.' She tried to extricate Joe from her legs; the Velcro on his slippers was fatal to tights. 'Everything he needs is in the pushchair bag. Get him to play group for nine and pick him up at twelve. Mum's coming from two till four and I'll be home at six. This is all in a note on the fridge.'

'Not Daddy!' moaned Joe, reaching to be picked up. Deb reminded herself that his daily bout of sobbing quietened minutes after the front door closed behind her. But David was shielding his eyes from the light. His face was clenched with pain.

'David? Oh no. I've got to go in – it's only my second week.'

'Just go then,' he said thickly.

'But you look awful. You know, I think it's stress.'

'Course it's not.'

'You went all quiet last night after Sarah called. What was it she wanted? Something about Uncle John?'

'Mmn.'

'And then she rang off because Jim got home?'

'S'got nothing to do with that.'

'I wish she didn't have to involve you. Look at you, David!'

'S'fine. Look, I'll walk him round to play group, then I'll crash.'

She had a heady moment of release: her day out in the world was not about to be snatched away. She'd soon be in the car with just her thoughts and the radio. 'If you're sure, then.' She bent to kiss Joe's head. 'Go to Daddy now, darling. Mummy will see you later.'

'No! No. No-o-o-o!!' Joe hurled himself to the floor, hammering with his fists and slippered feet. He began revolving, his kicks taking in her toes, the hall table, the phone wire and then the floorboards. 'Joe. Joe, stop it now.' She kept her voice low and authoritative, until a sharp kick connected with her ankle; then she let out a fishwife's bellow and Joe screamed harder, his body bucking at her feet.

'For fuck's sake!' David sat down on the stairs, his head in his hands. She was going to be late if she didn't leave now, but Joe's sobs were turning to choking sounds.

Mary was noticing so much more, as if life was running in her veins instead of sedatives. Like the precise quality of light and sound in the tower that meant it was time for Kim to come. Mary would find herself alert for her scuffing footsteps, picturing her chatter and warm touch. Steps at any other time meant him – and Mary heard them now, unusually quick. He was bounding up the stairs. *I need the deadness now; I need the pills.*

He came in and stooped to lock the door behind him. She noticed his vigour as he stood up straight, and the jolly way he turned to face her. Then everything stopped. She couldn't look.

'Who did this?' His heavy tread, then dark shoes by her chair. His sudden grip on her scalp was as sore as a burn. 'Who's had their filthy hands on you?' *Go inwards; don't be here for this.* But now she was flying off the chair and into the bed frame, her ribs crunching on metal. 'Who did this to your hair?' A quick glance revealed a fleck of spit on his cheek. 'What did you think? That you had somewhere nice to go? That you were getting away from me?'

He lunged on top of her, scrabbling at her nightdress and knickers. He grunted as he forced his way in, then huffed and gasped, hammering on and on. Teeth gritted. Unable to finish. Upset. It was a brutal age before he shuddered and subsided, then heaved himself off her. She flicked a look. Were those tears in his eyes?

'You heap of shit.' A sigh and a sniff. 'No nurses for a week. Keep that battered whore look to yourself. I'm in charge, Mary. I'm all you've got.'

He slapped at the light switch as he clattered out. She heard him retreating down the stairway, his breath shaky and loud. The hours of darkness lay before her, thoughts jabbering in her unmellowed brain. The present jagged and clear as a shard of glass. Past things rising from the cold earth to walk again.

There were voices outside the room where she lay, strapped down on the bed.

'But she's my wife.'

'She tried to murder your little girl!' John's harsh whisper. 'Trust me, I know these cases – this is not going to get better. Leave her here and I'll take care of her. Otherwise, the police will be involved. She'll end up in a prison or a secure hospital. Do you want that for her? No. We can save her from that.'

'What about the children?'

'She's a danger to the children. You must see that. Tell them she died tonight. Take them away and start a new life. Where they'll be safe. Come on now, Michael. Get a hold of yourself, for your children's sake. Come on.'

Footsteps going down the tower stairs. The two voices, one after the other; Michael's in peaks of agitation but then getting quieter and more hopeless – until it gave way altogether to John's persuasive drone.

'My children! They're taking my children!' Mary screamed into the night until her voice was torn. At last, more footsteps, and some staff burst in. 'I'm John Briers' sister! I'm not a patient!' she said. 'Please help me. They're taking...'

They were undoing her straps! They must believe her. But when she struggled to her feet, they flung her face down on the bed and twisted her arm behind her. Her nightdress was hauled up and a needle was stuck in her buttock with the force of a dart.

'The boss's sister, are you?' she heard someone laugh. 'That's a new one.'

She woke in sickly light, with John's face above her, his hands around her throat. Pain gagged her and a grey mist descended. *Let this be the end.*

But she was still in life's clutches when light came again. Her throat was broken and she couldn't speak. They came day after day with the injections. Her speech might have recovered, but there was nothing she could say. He kept coming to punish her for what she had shouted. A set of notes appeared with a strange name on them. Mary Greaves had not been near the clinic for years, and none of the staff knew her. She was Jane Grey to them: a patient who had once screamed out her delusions, but was now mute.

CHAPTER TWENTY-FOUR

35 weeks: Your baby is losing his wrinkled appearance and becoming plumper. You will be preoccupied about the birth now. It is time to think about your options for pain relief.

Stepping across the threshold of the Gatehouse, Sarah remembered how her footsteps used to quicken when she was coming home to Jim; their silly habit of clutching each other's hands through the letterbox as if they couldn't let a door come between them.

'Hey. You look knackered.' He got up from the sofa and came to take her briefcase. He was in jeans and a soft-lined lumberjack shirt, and the house was filled with the chemical whiff of a takeaway. She felt the moist spring of his lips, the brush of stubble. 'They shouldn't keep you so late.'

'It's just busy. I got on top of two deadlines and then Production came in about some urgent proofs that Rebecca hadn't checked. Her author's ringing me every ten minutes to complain about her.' As Jim took her hand, she heard her boss, Ruth's, parting comment, *Get yourself home, will you? No one expects you to wear yourself out!* So why did she stay away? The things she couldn't tell Jim stretched like a web between them, fibrous and dirty.

With a subtle movement, he turned her wrist and looked at the blood pressure monitor the doctor had advised her to wear. 'Sarah! It's a hundred and fifty over a hundred!'

'I told you, I've been busy. It'll go down.' Foil containers were piled on the coffee table on a greasy plate.

'That's really high!'

She sat down, breathing through her mouth to block out the metallic tang of the leftovers. 'Don't fuss – you'll make it worse.'

'It's not fussing. The job's taking too much out of you.'

She sighed. Work was a domain she could control, a relief from the nerve-rush that surged in her now. 'I'll feel better if you just sit with me. Would you rub my feet?'

'I think you should start your maternity leave now.'

'What? Have you any idea how much I've got to do before I go? I haven't had time to brief anyone yet, I've got...'

'You'll end up in hospital if your blood pressure gets any higher! Or have a stroke or something!' His accent had slipped into the sharp angles of the council estate.

Blood rushed in her ears. 'Oh, is that what you want? A little wife at home, like your mother?'

'Don't be stupid! I'm just thinking of you and the baby.'

'Well I'm not going to be your bloody mother!' What was she saying? She had lost the thread of her argument, and was raging at something inside her head. He turned to leave, and she sought for something stinging to call after him.

But he turned back. 'I don't know what's going on with you.'

'What do you mean? We always said I'd carry on working as long as I could.'

'But this could hurt our baby and you don't seem to care. This just isn't you, Sarah.' So much for his pretence, then – that she was still the same, that everything was going to be all right. She couldn't look at him. The room was full of the foul stink of the takeaway. 'I don't know you any more,' he said.

CHAPTER TWENTY-FIVE

Kim was wondering why she did this to herself as she rushed round, plumping cushions and picking bits up off the carpet (there wasn't even time to get the Hoover out). Hosting house group after a long work shift was enough to harden anyone's heart. You were meant to be sharing everyone's walk with the Lord but sometimes she found herself wishing they'd share a bit faster, then go home and let her get to bed.

But the first time the doorbell rang, it was Graham. 'I'm unfashionably early,' he said.

'Oh no, the others are always late,' Kim said, and caught herself sounding uncharitable. 'Mind you it is really hard to get a parking space round here.'

He opted for coffee and, in the spirit of a warm welcome, she fished out the good stuff from the back of the cupboard and began to make a pot. What was he thinking, sitting alone in her front room? It was starting to look so shabby – she hadn't kept on top of the decorating as Paul used to – but men didn't notice these things, did they? When she went back in, he was peering at the titles on her bookshelves. She was about to ask if he liked the same authors, but then heard a shuffling on her doorstep; the others had arrived.

Steve was leading the session, which was about forgiveness. After the Bible readings, they looked at some case studies that showed what a complicated subject it was. People's experiences were gradually drawn out of them. Jenna had smacked her daughter in anger years ago and it still haunted her. The group reassured her and came to the conclusion that it is important to forgive ourselves. Steve was struggling with anger towards his boss, who had belittled him in front of someone. Was Graham used to this kind of discussion? He made the odd comment, and nodded once or twice, but he didn't share much himself. The Bible he was weighing in his hand looked brand new.

Steve was asking for her thoughts. Talk about putting her on the spot in front of everyone! It wasn't compulsory to share. But she caught sight of Graham, looking at her with interest.

On a good day she could recite the story as though from a script. After twelve years of marriage that she thought had been happy, Paul had told her he was seeing someone called Julie. He was leaving her. Everyone had prayed that he would come to his senses, but he had pushed for a quick divorce and married Julie. For a long time, Kim told the hushed group, she had been unable to forgive. Her voice wavered on the words *devastated* and *hurt*. She swallowed and went on, describing how she went up for prayer ministry with Moira, and felt different afterwards, 'As though something inside me had lifted.' But that didn't begin to convey it. It sounded like the jargon that Tom called Christianese.

'But, did you actually manage to forgive them?' Ellie was new to the group, and newly married. Her eyes looked huge – with sympathy or perhaps alarm.

Kim was not so practised at telling the next part. She checked there were tissues in her bag. 'Julie got pregnant,' she said. 'And I made myself congratulate her, and ask her how things were going.' She remembered the recurring dream she had had that she was carrying Paul's baby herself. Waking up day after day, alone in the bedroom, her womb empty. 'One weekend Tom and Amy were at their Dad's as usual, but they came home early. Julie had been rushed to hospital. She lost the baby.' She was fishing a tissue out now. 'And I found that I was genuinely sorry. I sent her kind words in a card. And I really meant them.' *Weeping women, Graham's first time*, she thought. *He'll never come back*. She should have known not to finish the story. But then, how could she leave it unfinished? Because somehow, in the midst of it all, forgiveness had crept in, and even a scrap of love for this woman who had been her enemy.

'That was all a bit intense,' she said to Graham later, when the others had gone. 'Have you been to a house group before?'

'No, I just used to sit in the pew,' he said. 'I didn't really get into it that deeply. But thank you. It was good. Lovely coffee.'

'It is nice, isn't it? I should make it more often.'

'Have you been to that new coffee place?' he said. 'Next to the library?'

Kim searched her tired brain. 'I can't picture it. I don't get to town very often.'

'People keep raving to me about the coffee. It's from Monmouth, apparently.'

'I didn't even know they grew coffee in Wales!'

He chuckled. His jumper was blue and looked soft. It made his eyes seem very brown. 'Do you fancy giving it a go?' he said. It took her a moment to realise that he meant, with him.

CHAPTER TWENTY-SIX

36 weeks: You should be attending antenatal classes where you will get plenty of advice on labour and parenting. You may find that you develop a strong bond with other parents to be.

When she heard Joe clamouring to ring the doorbell, Sarah rushed to let him and Deb in.

'How's the working girl?' she asked from within Deb's tight hug.

'Fine! How's the lady of leisure?'

Sarah led them into the kitchen. 'Well, it's me, so it's not so much leisure as a programme of positive de-stressing. I do my pregnancy exercises to relaxation CDs. Then there's my book on taking control over harmful emotions.'

'How does that work, then?'

'You keep track of how many negative thoughts you have, and counter them with positive, productive ones. While drinking calming teas!' She opened a cupboard to reveal an array of boxes. 'Limeflower, chamomile, motherwort and lavender. Jim wants to know where I'm keeping my broomstick.'

Deb laughed. 'Who knew you could drink lavender. Do you want some, Joe?'

'No,' said Joe. 'It's horrid.'

'Hey Joe, guess what Auntie Sarah saw in the garden? Foxes! With big bushy tails. Shall we see what else we can find in the woods?'

Sepia cloud hung over the tree-tops as they set off through the garden gate, with Joe running lumpily ahead in oversized wellies.

'So – no regrets about leaving work?' Deb asked.

'No. I didn't want to, but things had got out of hand. At least I can look after myself a bit better now.'

'You seem to be doing really well.'

'Thanks. I'm trying. So how's it going, the agency managing?'

'Well, I felt a complete fraud at first, as if I'd raided the dressing up box for my suit. But I think I'm finding my feet. There's this office manager called Rhoda. She's been great at showing me how everything works, without making me feel stupid. I suggested a new way of doing something the other day. She went off and did it, and you know what – it actually worked!'

They strolled further into the November dimness of the woods, Joe making exploratory runs ahead of them, while Sarah shared the story of her last day at work. Earlier that week she had had to speak to Rebecca about her author's complaints. When everyone gathered round to present her with a card and gift, Ruth said, 'It won't be the same here without you.'

'No,' Rebecca said. 'Much less hormonal!' A spattering of laughter broke out; even Helen was smiling. Sarah thought of the sea-swell of worries that swept over her as soon as she left the office each day. She opened her giant leaving card and found that tears were falling onto the biro wishes, as if to prove Rebecca right.

'The cow!' Deb said. 'And I suppose everyone else thought it was a harmless joke – or that you'd had some sort of hissy fit with her?'

'Yes, that's exactly it.' Sarah felt the lingering burden of the story lift away. 'I've got to tell you,' she said. 'I've got a plan.'

'Sounds exciting!'

'Well, this relaxation business is all very well, but it doesn't get to the heart of what's stressing me. I still need to know what I'm really up against. And I can't rely on my uncle any more.'

The woods here exhaled a dank, rotten smell and beneath the trees, a patchy mist deadened all sound. They should have come to that big clearing by now, shouldn't they? Joe stayed nearby, dogging their steps as Sarah began to tell Deb about the hypnosis and how she'd remembered her uncle trying to get her into the nursery cupboard.

'Joe! Shall we play the doggy game?' Deb threw a stick far along the path, and he ran after it, giving Sarah time to get to the end of her story without him hearing.

'My God! So – that's all you remember? Nothing else has come back to you since?'

'No, but I don't want him near me any more. He's rung, but I've made excuses.'

'A bigger stick!' said Joe, stopping to turn over a long-fallen branch. Its underside was covered in bright orange fungus, and woodlice spewed out from a hole. He dropped it and backed away, big-eyed.

'What does Jim say?' Deb asked.

'Oh, I can't tell Jim! I promised him I'd drop all this. He'd have a fit if he knew. Don't tell him, will you? Or David. Promise?' In the fogged quiet, she heard the neurotic echo of her voice.

'No. OK.'

Something erupted from the undergrowth and flew at their heads. Joe cried out and Deb snatched up his hand as a fat woodpigeon beat the air, then fussed and settled on a branch overhead. They moved on quickly beneath the dripping trees, but Sarah was not at all sure now where they were going.

'In a way, I got what I wanted – I actually remembered my mother. She said, *Come on, snuggle up with me and we'll have a snooze.* I know, it's nothing, but I'm holding on to it! I'm going to find out what was wrong with her, and if it's in the family. And if David will help me, we can…'

'Oh, look… Maybe you should drop all this.'

'What do you mean? Why?'

'Well – for the sake of your health. And the baby's.' They had come to a tree lying on the ground, its trunk scarred and strangled by ropes of ivy. Joe ran to climb on it. They fixed their eyes on him.

'Look at me, Mummy, I'm on top! Look at me!'

'I know, darling, look at you!'

The fallen tree looked completely unfamiliar; Sarah had no idea where they were. 'But it's for the baby that I need to know.'

'Well, for David's sake then.'

'David? Why?'

'He keeps getting these terrible migraines. They knock him out for days. And even when he's not ill it's like he's … not with us.' Deb nodded towards Joe, who was scrambling down from the tree trunk. 'Today when I got home he just clung on to me, and I'm thinking, Why's he so traumatised when he's been with his Dad?'

They had stopped walking, and standing made Sarah ache. She went to perch on the fallen tree trunk. 'I didn't know.' David had resisted her search from the beginning, but she had just thought he was being his usual scoffing self. *I never think about it. It's in the past.* She stared at nut husks discarded by squirrels. 'Maybe it's trying to push everything back under the carpet that's making him ill.'

'He can't though, Sarah! You won't let him.' There was a hush under the winter skeleton of the canopy. Joe clamoured to be picked up, all his king of the castle joy gone. 'I'm sorry. I'm just worried about both of them.'

Cold moisture from the dead wood was seeping through Sarah's maternity jeans. When Jim asked later how their walk had been, she couldn't begin to explain.

The first stage of labour was underway, and the model cervix on the midwife's lap was opening. Sarah noticed Jim sharing conspiratorial glances with a man he had chatted to over coffee. He had delayed a work trip to come to the antenatal class. She pictured telling Deb and David, and all of them laughing at his spluttering reaction. But she couldn't ring, could she? Deb would think she was pestering David. The imagined laughter faded and died.

The parents-to-be sat on plastic chairs, surrounded by noticeboards. What a troubled world must pass through the hospital, in need of all these warnings and helplines.

'You've obviously done some reading,' Doctor Farnham had said at her appointment earlier, 'but the truth is, we don't know whether your mother suffered from hereditary mental illness.'

'But – in your opinion..?'

'I can't give an opinion without knowing your mother's medical history.'

'You mean I should try to get hold of her notes?' Sarah couldn't believe that she had not thought of this before. Who had been her mother's doctor? And what happened to people's medical notes when they died?

'No, I mean, you should be looking after yourself. We must keep an eye on your blood pressure and watch out for protein in your urine. But most importantly, you need to remain calm. I'm afraid if you can't reduce your blood pressure, we might need to admit you to hospital until your baby is born.'

Jim was nudging her. The model baby had finished its journey through the clacking plastic pelvis and was resting in the midwife's lap; the group had broken into chatter edged with hysteria. Sarah's neighbour was looking at her expectantly, obviously having asked her something.

'Sorry… I was miles away.' The woman looked down, too shy to persevere.

'All right?' Jim searched Sarah's face. She nodded. The night after her walk with Deb, she had wished she could just hold him and cry without explanation. Instead she lay beside him into the small hours, trying to rein in her racing pulse while he slept.

She looked at the women around her. All their worries about motherhood seemed to stop at the birth. Would she have decided not to have children if she had known the dilemmas facing her now? She tried to think rationally, but reason failed her; the baby was its own argument, snuggling inside her. It knew nothing of the world and its bleak noticeboards. She reached for Jim's hand, wishing a grasp could convey her quiet new conviction. She would do anything for it. Anything.

CHAPTER TWENTY-SEVEN

'What's this?' Deb said. There were two tickets stuck in the frame of the hall mirror.

David appeared from the living room. 'Tickets for the comedy club at the Scala. Thought we'd have a night out, like the old days. Have a drink. Go wild. Stay up after eight o'clock.'

There had been no word from Sarah, and he had lost his hunched look. She leaned over to kiss him and felt his lips hold hers. Children's television sent a pulse of noise from the living room. When David was in charge, it seemed to blare constantly from the corner.

'I'm home, Joe!' she called, and he trotted out, clutching his comfort blanket like someone emerging from a trance. 'Have you and Daddy had a nice day?' He leaned against her and she picked him up, kissing in the scent of his hair. As he rested his head under her chin, she looked at the tickets. Listening to the young nurses moaning about their hangovers, she had yearned for a time when she and David were always out at pubs, parties and comedy gigs. She had said something wistful when she got home. He must have been listening. 'Thanks, David! I heard about this on the radio – it sounds brilliant!'

'I thought so!' He stood with his arms folded, chin thrust out.

She felt a twinge of attraction. Might she have the energy for sex when Joe was in bed? Peering at the tickets, she noticed the date. 'Oh. Shit! It's the week Mum's away!'

'Shit!' Joe sat up straight and began to jiggle up and down in her arms. 'Shit!'

'It was the only date I could get,' David said. 'Can't Hilary babysit?'

'She's doing night surveillance for this new job of hers.'

'Well Sarah and Jim, then. They've always wanted to have him to stay.'

'I don't know.' Joe was wriggling wildly. She carried him into the kitchen and perched him on the worktop.

David followed her. 'What? Why?'

'Sarah seemed so stressed when we went for that walk. So kind of intense.' Looking up, she saw the photo booth shot of her and Sarah, grinning from the pinboard.

'Shit! Shit!' Joe began to pummel her with his feet.

'Joe, don't.' She lifted him down and he tried to clamber up her legs as though unsure if he wanted to hug her or hurt her.

'Well, this'll take her mind off things. She loves having Joe.'

'I don't know if it's a good time. She's really preoccupied.'

'Deb, listen to yourself. It's Sarah and Jim, for God's sake.'

She had bent his good mood out of shape. He had made an effort for the two of them, but he was turning away now, exasperated. 'Oh look,' she said, 'okay.'

'Yeah?'

'Yeah.' She kissed him, pressing a hand to the small of his back. 'You're right. Let's have a laugh together. Joe will be fine.'

'Can you pick up if you're there?'

The voice rang round the draughty spaces of John Briers' study in the tower. The room had rattling joinery and faded fittings, unlike his smarter office near reception, but it was out of bounds to clinic staff, and if they wanted him here, they rang. The computer here was not linked to the network, and he kept his own selection of paper files.

'Uncle John, are you there?' The voice was distorted by the answerphone, but still undeniably Sarah's: full, throaty and edged with need. His fingers twitched on the black folder in his lap, aching to reach for the receiver.

The hypnotism had been his masterstroke – conceived on the spur of the moment as she whined on, ironically, about not remembering her mother. Surely his 'something bad' prompt would release the memory of Mary's murder attempt. *Be careful what you wish for!* Since then, though, she had not responded to two messages of his, and for days the wound had lain rotting inside him, its pressure swelling. But now she wanted him. He could hear her breathing, and here in his lap were the pictures. He fixed his eyes on one from way back, near the beginning. The colours were faded but the details still had their effect. Her voice was impatient now – oh, she was used to getting her own way – but she couldn't conceal a pleading note: 'I still need that number, of my mother's doctor. Can you ring me back?'

The cheek of it. What was Mary to her, really? But over the hiss of the tape, he heard a sigh. He shifted in divine discomfort. A lesser man would deal with it himself, in seedy isolation, but he didn't have to sink to that. Sometimes he wished it were possible to write about it: the masterly way in which he ordered things and his musings upon it, which were often quite profound. But these things were unspeakable in the world outside. As the tape finished with a beep, he was fantasy-writing his memoir: 'A few steps away I had a female cut from the same cloth, for my satisfaction. One who could not resist me…' He let out a breath and felt his mouth stretch into a grimace of pleasure.

Mary pressed her forehead against the bars, breathing the cold odour of window glass and painted iron. She was held upright by muscles that were regaining their tone and a spine that was straightening.

'You worry about them, don't you?' Kim was arranging carnations in a plastic jug. 'You'd do anything for them.' She had been talking about Amy. Mary was glad the girl seemed better. What had Sarah been like at thirteen? What must she be like now?

Sarah had been the one who needed her. David was determined to be the big boy; he went to Michael's classroom after school and came home recounting the after-hours gossip he had eavesdropped: 'Miss Skinner's real name is Delia and her mother is going doo-lally.' He shrank from Mary's attempts to kiss him, and met her jollying brightness stony-faced. Perhaps he held it against her that at times she shooed him away, ruthless with panic because John was there.

But at four, Sarah still found an infant's comfort in her mother's closeness. Her face filled with anxiety at every parting. Mary could reassure her, light up her mind with questions or imaginings, make her laugh at silly things. Sarah was the one thing she had ever got right. She had a sensual echo of the warm weight of holding her, the salt-sweet smell of her skin. How could she have let that go?

The dark woods beneath her heaved in the winter wind and released a draught of memory.

She was searching for a cardigan she had left in the woods. She kept forgetting things lately. She'd ask Michael a question and go blank while he was answering. The other day had been their anniversary. They had sat opposite each other in the White Hart, but she had run out of things to say and drifted into the shadowland of thoughts.

'Well, I have tried to make you happy,' he had said, banging down his pint of bitter.

The cardigan was deeper into the woods than she remembered. How stupid that she still got that creeping feeling here; her heart jumped with every twig that cracked. Sarah would wake soon from her nap. Snatching up the cardigan, Mary walked fast, back towards the Gatehouse. Sweat stuck her blouse to her underarms as she opened the French windows. John had said he might come back. There were broken bits of leaf on the carpet, but they could have been there before; she was a useless housewife. She tipped her head, listening, but heard only her own annoying breathing. She crept into the hall and upstairs, her steps making virtually no sound. The quiet was like something holding its breath. Then a creaking sound, and his voice came from the nursery. 'Come on. It'll be our special hiding place. Our secret… Come on. Sarah?'

She could have knocked down the nursery wall, leaping and destroying like a wild creature. In the doorway, she thought a shadow moved. 'Sarah! Sa-rah!' Her voice was a shrill noise, sing-song and fake. But thumping footsteps sounded and there was Sarah, eyes anxious and bright, hair flying behind her. Mary took her hand and walked her away along the corridor, swinging her arm in a parody of playfulness.

But he was there behind them. He was probably furious. He never let her win.

'Jane? Are you all right?' The gnarled iron of the window bars was pressing against her forehead. An arm went round her shoulders, sticking her nightdress to her clammy skin. No one had been near her for days. She must smell. Gently, her fingers were prised from the bars. 'It's all right, Jane.' Kim stroked her upper arm.

She thought of the brimming bedpan only feet from where they stood. Kim took her arm away and chill air nipped where it had lain. Cold seeped hopelessly into her bones. She thought suddenly of all the pills she had hidden, in a tissue stuffed under her mattress.

'Look.' Kim was fumbling in a pocket. She took Mary's hand and tried to push something into it, but Mary's fingers were stiff. She couldn't grip. 'Please, try to tell me what's upsetting you.'

Sarah would be next. Mary had to warn her! But she couldn't even stand up. She let Kim guide her, trembling, to her chair and tip the pill into her mouth.

'I'll leave them for you.' *What? The carnations?* 'Look, you've been kind enough to listen to me going on. I'm here if you want to confide in me. I hope you'll find a way.' Kim's hand stilled the tremor in Mary's shoulder, and then there was the door closing, the scrape as the key turned. But no rattle. The rattle was the key being pulled out of the lock. John would be angry if he found it left in there again.

The tower night closed over Kim's footsteps, and Mary turned her head. Something lay on the table next to the jug of flowers. She hooked the pill out from the roof of her mouth, got up and stuffed it heedlessly in the tissue with the others. Then she sat down beside the table and picked up the notebook and pen.

CHAPTER TWENTY-EIGHT

On Thursday evening, Kim rang to finalise arrangements for Tom and Amy's stay at Paul's. When Julie answered, she sounded oddly elated – or perhaps just breathless, having run to pick up the call.

'Hi Julie. How are you?'

'Fine. Great actually – I'm pregnant again – fourteen weeks!'

'Julie! Oh. That's brilliant.'

'Yes! Everything's going well. We waited before telling anyone of course. And we'd like to tell the kids ourselves – do you mind keeping it a secret until we see them?'

'Of course not.' Words stumbled out. 'That's fantastic news! They'll be delighted! Well, Amy will. Tom will just grunt and shuffle – but underneath, for all we know, he'll be delighted.'

'Oh yes. The teenage thing. I guess I've got all that to look forward to!' For a split-second, Kim suspected the one-upmanship she used to read into Julie's every word. But no, surely she was just daring to look into the future after what she had lost. Kim's congratulations felt awkward, but she hoped they were warm.

She went to bed early, but then lay awake for hours. So that was why the Thai holiday had been suspended – Julie was in the early, uncertain days of pregnancy. That was why Paul had been tetchy when Amy pressed him about it. And when Kim spoke to Paul that time, he had been guarding Julie's secret. She was exhausted in the morning, as if she had spent the night struggling.

There was a blackboard at the new coffee place displaying a mission statement as well as the menu: *We aim to bring the Melbourne café scene to the garden of England.* It seemed a brave claim in the December drizzle, but Kim's cappuccino was creamy and full of flavour.

'I'm not even missing the chocolate sprinkles,' she said. 'Usually with cappuccino, I'm just in it for the chocolate.'

'I could ask for some?' Graham said.

'Oh no! They'd know I've never been to Melbourne. Oh. I needed that.'

'Work taking its toll?' he asked.

'Well, that too. I'm working in this psychiatric clinic in an enormous manor house. You walk miles. But I also had a dreadful night.' He regarded her with that searching look. He had talked quite a bit while they were waiting for their coffee, about his daughter as well as his teaching job at Ashbury College. 'I spoke to Julie,' she said.

'Your ex's wife?'

'Yes. You remembered! But then again it probably marked you for life, that house group.' She told him about the pregnancy and about lying awake going over it all. 'I hope I don't sound like some religious nutter,' she said, 'but it felt like this tussle between compassion and, well, the old jealousy.'

Graham nodded, but didn't seem to know what to say. She sipped her cappuccino. 'Anyway, this is really perking me up.' He asked about the clinic, and she told him a bit about Jane and trying to get her to communicate, though of course without using any names. Talk flowed – had she gone on too long? When he mentioned a TV programme he was reminded of, she turned the conversation to things he watched and films he liked.

They had got on to books when she caught sight of the clock.

'Oh, I'd better go! The kids will be home from school soon. They're off to their Dad's later.'

'Would they disapprove?' he said as they scraped back their chairs.

Were they worrying what their offspring thought, then? That would make this a date, wouldn't it? Not just friends from church meeting for coffee.

'I don't know,' she said. 'I said I was working.' She remembered that Graham's daughter had wanted him to go speed dating. Did she know they were meeting? Perhaps she would quiz him later about how it had gone.

It felt awkward saying goodbye. Perhaps it was just the sleepless night unnerving her. As she drove home, she wondered what Tom and Amy would think if they knew where she had been. Was there anything much to tell them, after all?

CHAPTER TWENTY-NINE

38 weeks: The baby's head may have dropped down into your pelvis. She is a perfect little newborn, just waiting for your hormones to activate contractions. She could be born any time between now and week 42.

Shampoo burned into Jim's eye, and when he reached for a towel, his hand flapped at an empty rail.

'Oh for –!' Couldn't one bloody thing go right? By the time he'd pressed a corner of his bathrobe into the smarting spot, the mirror revealed a pink stain over half the eyeball. How stupid was that going to look when he was out schmoozing Clarkson's mob later? He pictured the ribbing he would get from old man Clarkson – loud, high-handed and no doubt pissed.

Jim stood dripping in the warm fug, cleaning his teeth. How long, realistically, did he have to stay out with them? Clarkson had been known to demand they go on to Ashbury's one girly bar. Then as they watched the pole dancing, he would leer, 'You dirty bugger, Jim! What would your nice Sarah say?' His reflection looked bleak, peering out of the mist. Clarkson was small fry; the contract he might give them a consolation prize. Today they'd lost the Brigg Farm Estate, a tender Jim had been working on for a year. Twelve four-bedroom detached houses plus affordable housing, finally going ahead after a planning dispute – but the contract had gone to Rack & Webb. On Monday Jim would have to work out how their rivals had undercut Lawson's barely realistic, rock-bottom tender. It was the second job they had lost to them this year.

'Rack & Webb are just bigger players,' Brian had consoled him, feet on desk, after-hours, when they had worn the subject out. But they had all thought Jim's relationship with the developers was key. Steam clouded his face to a blur. It wouldn't be so bad if he could get somewhere in his own business. But two of his tenants had absconded without paying rent, and a couple of places he had spent time researching had turned out to be out of his league.

He padded along the hallway, draughts reaching the dampness beneath his bathrobe. That window wanted replacing, but it would need proper leading in keeping with the house. He pictured Lovett's look of strained politeness when he brought it up, as if he were a pestering child. Would the uncle ever sell the place? Why bother, if Jim would knock himself out adding value to it, with no guarantee of owning anything at the end? Staring into his wardrobe, he recalled the satellite dish quip and saw in a horrible flash the chav they took him for. That time at the clinic with Briers, he had even been wearing sports gear. Heat flared round his neck.

There had been no talk of buying the house since that day. Was Sarah disappointed? She didn't see the Gatehouse like he did: as part of a posh background, a moneyed past. That was the view from the council estate, he thought. She was so quiet lately. He thought of their excitement when they found out she was pregnant, how they had blundered through the flat in each other's arms.

His tie wouldn't go right; Jim flapped it undone and started again. When he first wore one for school, Mum showed him every morning, standing behind him to think the motions through. He had an odd flicker of memory, of being dragged away from her bedside. He had been so sure that she wanted him there, that she would call, *Come to Mum, Jimmy! Let him come to me!* But she just lay there all white-faced, saying nothing. He had heard the word 'breakdown,' whispered, but didn't know what it meant.

The nursery door swung in on gentle lamplight. Sarah was on the sofa bed, reading to Joe. He was tucked up under the duvet in his Thomas the Tank Engine pyjamas.

'There was once a baby with no mummy...' Between the lulling, rhythmical phrases of the story, she turned her head and let her lips touch the boy's hair. She looked sleepy herself, the skin under her eyes puffed and dark, but there was something confident about her, as though she did this every night. Jim took in the strange comfort of the tale, wishing he didn't have to leave.

Sarah had taken Joe's breakfast order over the phone: 'I doesn't like cor-flakes, I likes chocolate balls'. Searching the supermarket aisles, she had felt a soft movement inside her, of weight adjusting downwards like a docking in her pelvis. Her book said it meant the head was engaged and the birth was only weeks away.

She was relishing the smell of Joe beside her – all baby shampoo and bodily warmth – when he surprised himself with a loud fart, and laughed in delight.

'You pickle! Look, Uncle Jim's come to say ni-night.'

'Sorry I've got to go, you two,' Jim said. 'I'd tell Clarkson where to stuff his night out – but I'd get the boot, and we'd be poor. Ni-night Joe. Night, big girl.' He kissed them both. 'You look sleepier than him.'

A huge yawn slurred her words. 'I'm fine. Don' think I'll be far behind him, though.'

'You sure this is OK?'

She nodded. 'We'll be fine.' He gazed at the two of them, his face relaxing for the first time since he came in from work. Then he stood up to go; the shift in his weight rocking the bed.

She had not been in her own bed long when an explosive crackle close to her ear sharpened into Joe's whimpering. The baby monitor's red lights lit up in a row. She went in to find him rigid, staring past her at the darkness of the hallway.

'What's the matter, darling?'

'I doesn't likes it!'

'What don't you like?' The back of her neck prickled at the sight of his huge black pupils.

'In the woods. The big bad.'

'There's nothing bad here Joe. Just Auntie Sarah and your nice warm bed.' She curled up beside him in the night-light glow and watched as his breathing settled and his thumb dropped, glistening, from his lips.

In her own bed again, she turned the baby monitor to face her, straining to listen. Was that noise from the speaker, or just the racing of blood in her ears? It didn't feel right, with a child in the house, to release her grip on consciousness. But the sound was just the usual woodland rush, like waves at the seaside, and tiredness was rolling over her; she could not get up again if she wanted to. Her body cast her adrift; perceptions fogged and distorted. She sank further under the duvet, thoughts unravelling into impressions, then dispersing into deep, disabling sleep.

She was walking through the woods in leafy sunshine. Mary stepped from behind a tree, smiling. She had a baby in her arms, as tiny as a doll. Sarah wanted to run to her, but then she saw how ghastly pale she was. Mary was dead! What was this mother thing? The woods around her were dank and decaying and as Sarah looked, Mary's smile faded; her eyes went hard. Trees were falling around them with a crashing sound. Mary had a demon's face and was stepping towards her. Sarah tried to run but her legs were nightmare heavy. She made herself stop and squeeze her eyes tight shut.

She awoke in her room. There was a reverberation like the moment after a noise. She sat up. Was that something downstairs? Dream-muddled, she dragged herself out of bed, bumped her belly on the doorframe, then padded past the quiet nursery and down the stairs. Perhaps Jim had forgotten his key? The porch light showed no one on the doorstep. But there – a thumping sound, just as the wind roared through the trees. Surely Joe couldn't have got outside? She made herself head along the hallway and peer round the doorframe into the living room.

Outside the French windows was a woman in white, staring.

Sarah screamed. Recognition flared up and wavered. A crackle upstairs swelled into a wail. Joe! She looked back at the French windows. No one was there. There was crying and she ran for the stairs. Joe was at the top, wild-eyed.

'Joe!' She heaved herself up towards him. He screamed and in slow motion tottered and fell. She flashed a hand out and grabbed him. Flailing, off-balance, she gripped the banister and stopped them both from falling. 'Joe! Joe! Shh! It's OK!' She grasped him to her and carried him upstairs, but he shrieked and flung himself about. When she put him down on the landing, he dragged himself away from her. 'Joe it's me! It's Auntie Sarah!' But he cowered before her and wailed.

'I wan' mummy. I wan' mummy.' Joe crouched in their bed, giving tiny hiccupping sobs, his eyes drooping with tiredness.

'Mummy's coming, mate. She'll be here soon.' Jim paced to the window for the umpteenth time, but there was nothing but blackness outside.

'I wan' mummy.' Jim stroked his head. When Sarah had tried this, it had caused a further burst of screaming.

'So – you had a nightmare and woke him up?'

Jim was heading for the window again.

'I've told you, he cried, so I stayed with him and settled him down. He was fast asleep when I left him. Then I woke up and thought I heard a noise downstairs. I went down to look and … I saw this woman outside the French windows… '

'What woman?'

'Well that's the thing – I had this weird moment – I was sure it was my mother.'

He looked at her as Joe had looked into the darkness at bedtime. 'For fuck's sake, Sarah!'

Joe began to wail. A light swept the room, making a black shape of Jim and sending his shadow raking across the bed.

'What?' said Sarah. Her legs were trembling.

'Your mother's dead!' Heat rushed in a shivery wave to her skin. Car doors slammed and now footsteps crunched in the gravel. The doorbell pierced the quiet.

The comedy was in full flow and Deb was helpless, face screwed up, when Jim's text came. She rang him from the lobby. Joe was upset – something about a nightmare. Jim and Sarah couldn't console him. They had better come.

'I'm sure it's nothing,' David said in the car.

'They wouldn't have called us for nothing.' She felt snatched from the joyous abandon of earlier, her coping skills off-kilter after a couple of drinks.

But nothing had prepared her for the sight of Joe in Jim and Sarah's bed. He was sickly pale, his breath shaking, and he couldn't tell her what was wrong. Sarah put out a hand to him, but he cringed away. Deb snatched him up. She felt the heat of him; his chest heaving, his little heartbeat like a bird's against her ribcage.

'Hi Sarah,' David said. 'What's up?'

'Let's just get him home,' Deb said. She walked out without a word to Sarah.

She stood in the Gatehouse living room. Joe was holding her fiercely, as if he was trying to climb inside her.

'Seems like Sarah had some kind of nightmare,' Jim was saying. 'She screamed, and Joe woke up. I s'pose, finding himself in a strange house, he just got really scared.'

'He's still frightened now.' Deb looked at David standing in the doorway, not meeting anyone's eye. As the night-time chill cooled Joe's pyjamas, she realised something else. 'He's wet!'

'Nappy must've leaked,' David said.

But Deb knew the intimate scents of their child. 'It's not that. It's sweat. And he's cold.'

Jim grabbed a fleece to wrap round Joe. His voice was hushed.

'Sarah hasn't been herself. She said she'd let this Mary thing go, but I think she's been ringing her uncle again…'

'She hasn't let it go!' Deb burst out. 'She's been pestering David for all sorts.'

'Deb…' David's look of reproach was like a needle piercing a boil.

'I didn't know that.' Jim sank down on the sofa. 'I think she feels she needs to get things straight before the baby's born.'

'Well she's going a funny way about it! She got this Uncle John to hypnotise her. Did you know that?!'

In the silence that followed, Deb walked out of the house. She buckled Joe into his car seat and sat beside him in the back, her arm held over his middle as he fell into exhausted sleep. Eventually, David came out too. The woods were black and seething, whipping past their windows on the long way home.

CHAPTER THIRTY

38 weeks: It is important for you to choose how and where you will give birth. Don't listen to other people's scare stories. Your midwife will reassure you and discuss your birth plan with you.

Joe's bed creaked as she laid him down – its slats were broken where he jumped on it – but he did not wake up. She was aware of David lurking behind her.

'Can you get me some clean pyjamas? I'll bath him in the morning.' David looked baffled and started looking through drawer after drawer, wrenching the rickety chest. She pointed, exasperated, 'In there.'

She switched off the main light and touched the base of the Toy Story lamp to its softest setting. Joe's head lolled on the pillow, his lips slightly open, lashes resting on his cheeks. She began to remove the damp Thomas pyjama top, pulling it up over his chest and then lifting his arm to get to the sleeve. She turned to see if David had found a clean one – how had he never learned where things were kept? When she turned back, the top had cleared Joe's shoulder. Around his arm was a storm-cloud of bruising.

'David!' She slapped at the lamp base and light revealed the livid injury. David looked dumbly at her before following her gaze. 'Oh my God!' she said. 'I said we shouldn't leave him with her!'

'What do you mean? Sarah wouldn't hurt him!' But blood was pooling in the soft tissue of Joe's arm. When he cried earlier, he must have been in pain. 'You can't think that!' David tossed the clean top on the bed. 'She's your best friend! She wouldn't hurt anyone!'

'I bet that's what they said about your mother!'

'How can you say that?' The sinews stood out in David's neck. *Oh, now you're angry?*

'Just get out!' she hissed, shoving the wet top at his chest. 'Let me look after him!'

Kim hauled herself up the tower steps, having woken, disbelieving, to her alarm. With the kids at their Dad's, she had agreed to a Saturday shift, but she had had another bad night. What had she been thinking, going on about Julie's pregnancy to Graham? She had lain awake, sure that she had messed things up. She shuddered, reliving their conversation. Had she actually told him she was still jealous? Perhaps it had just been a friendly coffee. Whatever it was, she had blown it.

She leaned on the tower wall and felt in her pocket for the key. But it wasn't there. Had she left it in the door again? The lock was an empty hole. Befuddled, head thudding, Kim made herself stop and think. The orderlies had their own sets of keys, kept at their station in the basement. She turned and headed downstairs.

She came back later, full of things to tell Jane, but when she opened the door, the window chair was empty. The bedding covered a motionless mound. Just inside the door, Kim felt an obstruction through the flat sole of her shoe. Crouching, she picked up the inner tube of a biro, bent in the middle. Alertness cut through the fog of fatigue – you could self-harm with the parts of a biro. She recalled Jane clinging to the window bars, agitated. There had been pinpricks of dried blood in her scalp. Had she been pulling out her hair?

'Jane?' There was no answer from the bed, but the covers rose and fell with peaceful slowness. On the table by the window, Kim found the plastic casing of the biro; it was intact, with no jagged breaks. She straightened out the inner tube, pushed it back in and capped it. She picked up the notebook and flipped through it, hope fluttering with the pages. It was blank.

Feeling so tired, it went against the grain to disturb someone's sleep. Kim reached under the bed for the bedpan. She would sort this out and come back later.

Mary pulled back the covers as the footsteps receded down the stairs. She ran her hands through her hair and bits of twig and leaf showered on to her pillow.

The night seemed unreal now, like a dream, or one of their childhood games. She had pushed a notebook page through the gap at the bottom of the door, then used the inside of the biro to push out the key. She had heard it fall and feared it had bounced out of reach, but when she pulled the paper back into the room, it was there. *Escape Plan Thirteen!*

She had made her way out and across the grounds, bracing herself every step for a shout of discovery. Branches and brambles had grabbed at her nightdress in the black night of the woods. She had clutched at her hair, remembering the bat, the demons. *I'm not a child any more. I'm not a captive.* She still knew the place for their secret hole in the fence, but time had grown over the route; she had to fight through undergrowth where she and John had walked freely along a path. All the way through the woods, she had thought of what she would say. Knocking at the French windows, she had seen a woman with tumbling curls and her little girl's face. She had tried to call out to her, but a thicket had grown over her voice. And then the screaming. Mary had stumbled back through the garden. How stupid she had been. She couldn't help anyone, and where could she go now – an escaped lunatic, voiceless, useless? She would be discovered and dragged back to the clinic. Sickness rose from her belly at the thought of his punishment; dizzy and weak with it, she leaned against the gate. She might as well slink back of her own accord, and hope he never found out.

Mary crouched on her knees, scrabbling at the woodland debris and throwing handfuls under the bed. Sarah's scream rang in her ears. Her fingers paused, trembling, in her hair. She was the night-time terror, the demon in the woods – the opposite of all that she should be to her children. 'I can't do this any more.' She slumped over, her mouth hanging open. 'You have to, for Sarah.' She thought of the old habit from school; John as a shepherd with a tea-towel on his head and her clomping in plimsolls, being an angel. *Hands together and eyes closed.* She had stopped all that years ago; you couldn't tell God what happened to the angel in the dark.

'Please God, please,' she said, weeping, snot hanging from her nose. Her head sank onto the pillow and she lay in a foetal curl: 'For Sarah – help me for Sarah.' She saw her through the window again, curly-haired and lovely. She said, 'Thank you.' A calm – or just exhaustion – came over her and she sank into its mercy.

The Gatehouse rang with emptiness, like somewhere abandoned after a disaster. All Sarah could hear was the creaking of the stairs, the dry whisper of her hand on the banister rail. How had she slept at all? On the bottom step she saw herself reaching the same spot the night before and overhearing Deb:

'She got this Uncle John to hypnotise her. Did you know that?!'

The living room was brightly lit by slanting winter sunshine. There were cushions scattered everywhere from a camp Joe had been making. She had chuckled at herself, watching him wreck her precious tidiness.

Joe's special cereal stood waiting on the kitchen table. She had pictured Deb and David arriving to find them all eating together, and staying to chat about their evening and the funny things Joe had said and done. Where was Jim? She must try to explain to him. But there was a note on the table: *Gone out. Back later. Jim.*

Back in the living room, the red light of the answerphone was flashing. She pressed the button and Jim's voice burst out:

'Sorry, I didn't pick up in time... Stupid machine!' The answerphone had recorded his conversation at the same time as playing the 'leave your message after the tone' speech, which now partly obscured a second voice.

'… Sarah's uncle… just responding to your enquiry… everything all right?'

'… just had a bad night.' Sarah struggled to hear as the speakers interrupted each other, battling the cacophony of the recorded message.

'I hope Sarah is all right? She was … stressed indeed… when I last...'

'... needs some peace and quiet...'

'... if I can be of any assistance. There is help if she would only... We have the facilities here at Woodlands to …'

A beep blared out. Sarah's skin burned hot, then chilled. As the machine fell silent, the tight weight of the baby shifted inside her, disturbed.

It was over an hour later when the back door opened.

'Where've you been?'

'We needed milk,' Jim said. 'I had a walk through the woods to the shop'. But it took only forty minutes to walk to the village and back. As he opened the fridge, they both saw the carton already lying on the top shelf. 'Oh.' He shut the door. 'You all right?'

'There was an answerphone message. I heard you and Uncle John talking about me.' His gaze slid away from her.

'We weren't talking about you. He called and I didn't get to the phone in time –'

'Why would he call you?'

'He was ringing me back. I rang him the other day to talk about our situation here...' What did that mean – their situation? She saw him making the call with that look he had had the previous night. 'I mean us not having a tenancy agreement – or any kind of status. I asked if he'd consider selling to me... To us.' Sarah pulled out a chair and sat down, leaning on her hands. How could he be thinking about property in the middle of all this?

'Sarah..?' He touched her shoulder. She flung out a hand towards the living room.

'It sounds like you two were plotting to have me carted off to Woodlands.'

He crouched in front of her, then stood and leaned over; there seemed no comfortable way for them to be together. 'How could I do that? Sarah? I love you. You're having our baby.'

'The way you looked at me last night. As if I'd lost it.'

'I'm sorry. I love you,' he said again, but he looked tense and miserable.

It was past nine in the morning, but Joe was still asleep, knees up under him, face wedged sideways on the pillow. Part of Deb wanted him awake, being his normal self so that she could see that he was all right. But this way she could sit on the end of his bed without having to do anything. She was a battered shell, just holding together around a chasm of tiredness.

David had not come to bed. He must have gone to his attic room sofa-bed as he did when Joe was having a bad night. If he apologised, she might say sorry too for shoving him and shouting. She got up almost without meaning to as she thought through the conversation they would have. A monster truck lay on a middle stair and she pushed it aside with her foot. She had been so pleased when he organised the evening out.

She found him standing in the kitchen with his back to a pile of unwashed plates and saucepans. Brightness poured sideways through the dirty window, giving everything the significant look of a photograph. David was wearing the same clothes as the night before. He looked as if he might come towards her, but then hung back like a big, sullen boy. As useless as he had been last night.

'I can't do this on my own any more, David. I thought that when I went back to work, you'd come down from your bloody ivory tower and be a proper Dad.'

'I am a proper Dad. I look after Joe!' She saw his shock. She was forcing him from cover.

'You've been like a zombie ever since Sarah started with all this Mary stuff.'

'Do you think I wanted that? Do you think I went looking for it?!'

'Well then, let her get on with it, and stop getting involved!'

'I'm not involved! I don't want to be!'

'Why do you pander to her then? She's just starting to leave you in peace – why does she have to have Joe just because she wants to? And the minute you left the room after seeing his bruises, you were straight on the phone to her!'

'To find out what had happened! And it was Jim I spoke to, not Sarah. I explained to you about her catching him when he fell.'

True, she had been relieved to hear an explanation for the bruises; it had allowed her finally to go to bed. But she would not let go of the sweet, violent flow of her outrage. 'I know that. But something is not right with Sarah, and she's trying to suck you into it.' She slumped into a kitchen chair. 'And it's got to stop. I've had enough.'

'You've had enough!?' There was a teaspoon in his hand and he smashed it on the draining board with a great crash of crockery. He swept past her. A moment later, a slam reverberated through the house. She sat staring at the draining board, wondering if anything was broken.

Deb came to much later, aware of a change in the room. Joe was leaning against her side. They had had breakfast together after he woke up; Joe had been little subdued and she was keen to behave as normal, but was quietly watchful. After a game with his cars, with a muttered, sing-song commentary, he had asked for his favourite DVD, and they had snuggled up on the sofa. She must have sunk into sleep before the titles finished.

David was standing over them, his hair dishevelled. Behind him on the television, a purple bear and a green dinosaur were singing a cheery song. Was he here to shout in retaliation? Or to pack his things? Maybe he would want to carry on as before. Her throat tightened.

'Come to Daddy?' He was reaching out to Joe, whose head made a nodding movement against her side. David planted his hands carefully under his arms, then sat down next to Deb with him on his lap.

The three of them gazed at the highly coloured characters singing the alphabet and dancing.

'I know I just stood there last night, like an idiot,' David said. 'It's that house.' The song reached an annoying crescendo.

'The house? I thought you didn't remember it?'

His eyes were full and shining. Deb had never seen him shed a tear, not even when his father died. 'I remember Mum leaning over Sarah, telling her to go back to sleep. Then she was pushing down with a pillow… there was this thudding noise… I was on my knees screaming for Dad. Then footsteps came running and the door opened. And I could see what she was doing…'

'Oh God, David. I'm sorry.'

David hand pressed Joe's head against him, the caress blocking his ears. 'How frightened must he have been? Waking up in that dark house, hearing screaming? And us not there when he needed us? And me… You're right. I am no bloody use.'

The bear and the dinosaur fell in an exhausted heap and laughed.

'I didn't mean that. I just want you with us.' Deb sank closer to him, wanting his warmth, but his skin, where it touched her, was freezing.

'I am going to be a proper Dad,' he said. I don't want him to have bad memories.'

'What about Sarah?'

'She'll have to go on without me.' Joe leaned back into the two of them and settled down.

CHAPTER THIRTY-ONE

Kim didn't usually keep her phone with her when she was working, but she had slipped it into her uniform pocket that morning, telling herself that Tom and Amy might text her from Paul's. As she headed back to the tower for the third time that day, she remembered saying to Graham how far you walked in this job. If only she had stuck to talking about work! She must have come across as someone who can't let go of the past. Well, Paul and Julie were moving on. Amy would be getting excited about being a half-sister. Tom was choosing A level subjects and thinking about applying for university. In the blink of an eye, he would be gone.

Her phone vibrated against her hip, and she stepped into the quiet space at the bottom of the tower staircase. She didn't recognise the number. *I enjoyed coffee,* the text said. *Do you fancy doing it again? I'm not around Sunday but could do same time next week? Graham*

Kim stood in the dimness, smiling. The kids said you looked needy if you replied straight away. *I enjoyed it too,* she typed back. *That would be lovely.* Graham had been so straightforward. She liked that about him. She pressed 'send' and bounded up the stairs.

Jane was sitting in her window chair.

'Oh, you're up! I left you to sleep before. You looked so peaceful.'

Her stare was fixed on the trees as usual, but there was something about her today: a trembling quality, as though some of her statue-like rigidity had melted away.

'Let's get you washed, and I'll change this nightie. It looks a bit the worse for wear. Is that a grass stain? Oh, did Mr Briers take you out in the grounds? Good idea. Put a bit of colour in your cheeks.' Then again, she had never known Jane to leave this room. The nightdress had probably not been washed properly before it came to her.

She had been going to tell Jane about Julie's pregnancy, but it seemed less pressing now. Instead she kept a close eye on her as she tidied and did her usual checks, wondering what it was that had changed. There were no medical signs you could write on a chart.

But she looked more alive – or was it more vulnerable?

Kim crouched in front of her, holding one of her hands. She pulled the notebook and pen towards them on the table. 'Jane, if there's anything I can do for you or anything you want to tell me, I'm here for you.' The face remained averted. Kim stood up, and gave Jane's shoulder a final press as she went to turn away. She felt a shifting under her touch, and then the gentlest of pressure. Papery fingers covered her hand, and for a couple of heartbeats, the blue eyes looked right into hers. Then Jane's gaze was back on the window, her hand sinking back into the stillness of her lap. 'Well, I'll see you again tomorrow,' was all Kim said. 'I'm around all weekend.'

Kim still felt a flutter of awe as she made her afternoon rounds of the ground floor of West Wing. Things seemed to be changing at last after moving with glacial slowness for so long. She leaned over to hand a pill tub to Quentin, a thin, sombre man in his forties. His skin was so pale that she could see the tracework of blue veins across his temple.

'Quentin?' His expression was fixed on the floor with forlorn intensity. Kim touched his arm and leaned closer, into a rancid smell coming from his head. His pillowslip must be in dire need of changing. 'Quentin, are you all right? It's Kim. We used to chat? Do you remember? I haven't been for a while. I've been over in the East Wing.'

Quentin looked up at her, dazed. 'Oh. Yes I – yes. Kay?'

'Kim. You told me about your Mum, and her coffee mornings.'

He nodded. 'I miss her very much.'

'Yes. You had a good life together, didn't you? I remember how sad you were when we talked.'

'I can't seem to shake it.

You weren't supposed to sit on the beds, but there was no chair; Quentin, like many of the patients, didn't have visitors. Kim sat down beside him and her bulk shook the mattress beneath his spindly frame; he had a weightless look, like a dried-out husk.

'I'm sorry. Are you still feeling low?' There was a stale, warm stench coming from the bedclothes. He bowed his head as though it were too heavy to nod.

Grief had brought Quentin to Woodlands at great expense to his busy, well-to-do relatives, but here it had consolidated into long-term despair. How was he to recover his spirits in this stinking room? 'Your pills, Quentin.' Kim put the tub in his hand, wondering if the drugs did anything more than blunt his emotional reactions, making him less trouble to the staff. She stood up to pour him water, but the jug was empty, so she went over to the sink. 'I think we could cheer this place up a bit, Quentin. I'll find you a chair to sit in during the day, and some nice fresh bedding. Have they not been round to wash you this morning?'

'You're the first person I've seen.'

What were the orderlies thinking of? Kim stalked over to his cupboard, telling herself that it wasn't their fault; they were poorly paid, understaffed and not properly trained.

'Oh, that's not good, is it? I hope you'll have some more company soon. Reverend Benson is letting a group of volunteers come from my church. They're going to help the orderlies and visit some of the patients. They should have more time to talk. Oh – the cupboard's bare.' Kim went and looked along the corridor. A few doors away, a sleepy-looking youth was carrying a bucket and mop.

'Excuse me!' she called. 'There's no spare bedding in this room.'

He gave a sideways nod. 'S'in the stores.' He turned and continued on his way.

'Quentin, I'm going to pop and get you some clean bedding. I'll come straight back and we'll have a proper chat. Okay?'

'Yes. Thank you. I'd like that.' His gentle politeness took her back to their previous conversations. Shc had started bringing coffee and biscuits, in honour of treasured memories of his mother. As he watched her leave, his face held a new alertness.

Kim hurried along the corridor. Her shift should have ended, but it didn't matter; Tom and Amy wouldn't be home until Wednesday night. Why not try to make a difference for Quentin? After all, she seemed to be on a roll.

The door the orderly had indicated opened on to a short flight of steps, descending into a windowless corridor. She looked around for something to prop the door open with, but there was nothing. It swung shut behind her with a thud.

She walked on utilitarian lino, under bright strip lighting, thinking of Quentin's expectant face. *Lord, please heal him. And let me help him. In fact, I want a miracle. I want him out of here.* She came to an unmarked door and pushed it to reveal a store for cleaning equipment. The next one was piled up with furniture. Where did they keep the bedding, for goodness sake? At last she spotted a door marked 'Linen Store,' and quickened her footsteps.

Before she reached it though, she stopped. Beside her in the neon glare was an old door like the one leading to the tower: unpainted and unmarked. It was open just a crack, revealing another corridor leading straight ahead; this one unlit. She could just see a door on the left. A distant rumbling made her start, and then – were those footsteps? The noise sharpened into a rattle. She let out a loud breath as an orderly approached along the bright corridor, pushing a trolley. It was one of the clinic's few old-timers. He opened the door to the linen store and disappeared inside.

'Reg!' It was a moment before he came out, laden with tea towels. She pointed to the dim space beyond the door. 'There's no one in there, is there?'

'No. Hasn't been used for years, far as I know.' He walked away with an arthritic gait, using the trolley as a walking aid. Usually you could not stop him from chatting. Kim had an urge to hurry after him, but he was moving surprisingly quickly.

She stared into the unlit corridor as the echoes of the trolley died away. There was a faint outline of light around the door on the left. Stepping closer, eyes adjusting, she saw that it was not quite closed. She pushed at it and went inside.

A crack of daylight from a blind over a high window shed the only light. Kim blinked and stared, taking in another door in the wall to her right. In front of her was a narrow bed with thick restraining straps. Beside it stood a heavy wooden chair, also with straps. Like the electric chair, she thought, for executions. Something glinted and she could just make out a trolley containing hypodermic needles and archaic-looking medical equipment. What was this? A disused room? A monument to the history of asylums? By the bedside though, was a modern lamp. And the bed was made up like the ones upstairs. Laid out across it was a hospital gown. She picked it up and stared; it looked brand-new. And there, where the gown had been, was a rectangle of black.

Kim reached out and flipped open a folder. Thumbnail photographs, twelve on an A4 page: a woman being treated in a bed and in a chair; the room oddly familiar. Old records? Then she lifted up the file, and saw the gown pulled aside, legs strapped apart, breasts exposed, and there on the anguished face, lipstick the colour of dried blood.

A hand gripped her arm.

'What are you doing?' John Briers looked down at the folder in her captured hand, and then back up into her eyes. The folder dropped on to the bed. 'I think we have some things to discuss,' he said. He let go of her and took a few quick steps back into the dimness. She thought, He's going to march me out of here and sack me. She saw herself running into the light towards her car. But then she heard him close and lock the door.

CHAPTER THIRTY-TWO

'Houston, we have a problem.' Rhoda came through into Deb's office, a partitioned section of an airy room in a Georgian house with a sweeping view of the town.

'Already?' Deb had barely had time to start up her computer. Rhoda had been secretary of the agency since it started, and was happy to share her invaluable knowledge with Deb; but she also liked to tell lengthy stories, full of drama and speculation.

'I know, talk about the Monday morning from hell! They've dismissed another of our nurses from the Woodlands Clinic.'

Rhoda plonked a file on Deb's desk.

'Woodlands?' Deb called up the client list and typed in a search. She had noted the name when she first went through the CareCorps files. A screen listed the nurses contracted to Woodlands. 'Which nurse?'

'Kim Saunders. She's the fourth we've had dismissed from that place. And she has always had a glowing reputation.' By this time, Deb was looking at the notes in red after three of the names: *Contract terminated by client.*

'Have they given a reason?'

'I spoke to a Stephanie Walters, Kim's line manager. She said she'd booked in some extra weekend shifts, but she didn't turn up for work yesterday or today.'

'Surely that's not grounds for instant dismissal?'

'Apparently the order came from John Briers, the Director.'

'Really? Why would he be involved?'

'Kim worked with a patient in his direct care. The staff nurse didn't sound that surprised. Almost as if she'd seen it coming...'

'So what does Kim have to say?'

'I've left messages on her home phone and her mobile, but I can't get a reply. You'd think she'd be keen to give us her side of the story.'

'She might be ill,' Deb said. 'Noro virus is doing the rounds, isn't it? Let's see if we can speak to her later.' She hoped her words had an air of finality, but Rhoda stood with arms crossed, gazing out of the window, where rainclouds had blown in after the weekend's cold, clear skies.

'I wouldn't mind, but four nurses! It just doesn't happen anywhere else. And all good nurses we've had no other problems with. Well, Kyle Hayes was a bit of a party animal, he might have been turning up with a hangover. But even with him – no issues anywhere else.'

Deb saw Rhoda open her mouth to start again, and jumped in, 'Why don't you ring the clinic and ask for clarification on the grounds for dismissal. It can't just be two days' non-authorised leave. Then we'll see where we stand.'

'Right! Yes. I will.' There was an excited look in Rhoda's eyes, and she hurried back to her office.

Deb pulled Kim Saunders' file towards her and flipped through her CV, work record with the agency, and contracts, including that with Woodlands. The blue band at the top showed that this had been adapted from the CareCorps standard contract; some private clinics altered the terms. Deb's gaze came to rest on the line: 'Dismissal at the Director's discretion'. CareCorps didn't have a leg to stand on. She was about to take the contract into Rhoda's office, but found herself staring at the door. Was Sarah's uncle a shady character – a danger to children, even? Did Deb have a professional duty to report him? On what evidence, though, other than a memory under hypnosis? And Woodlands was an adult clinic; he had no children in his care. But vulnerable people... Her mind ran in circles. There had been no mention of Sarah in their house since Saturday; though Deb kept thinking of things she would usually tell her. On Sunday afternoon, David had taken Joe out to a play area. He had come back glowing and settled down to show Daddy one of his puzzles. David was talking about taking him to the Science Museum: 'I saw how he did that robot puzzle. He's a scientist just waiting to happen.'

Rhoda walked into her unfocused stare. 'I've just spoken to someone on reception at Woodlands. She didn't know about the dismissal – I could hear her asking someone else about it. Then she just said it was Mr Briers' orders, for the two days' absence and unsatisfactory standards of work. But I heard this other woman say that Kim's car is still there. They said she must have left it when she went home on Saturday evening.'

'Why would she do that?' A draught from the window crept down the back of Deb's blouse. 'You might fancy a walk through the woods on a summer evening – but in December? In the dark?'

'No, and I'm not being funny but it is a psychiatric clinic – what if something happened with one of the patients? I mean, what if she never left?'

'But then why would Briers dismiss her?'

'I know! I've been thinking about Divina Santos. Briers sacked her last year. I had her up here in tears, saying she was sure you get kicked out there for asking too many questions.'

'Questions about what?'

'Poor standards of care, she said. Over-medicated patients. And anything about the boss. I thought we should look into it but Sian said Divina could be a drama queen and we didn't want to alienate a good client. But that was before the other three were dismissed.'

Rain sounded, gusting against the window. Rhoda went back to her office to make some calls, and Deb opened an email and stared at it without taking anything in. Was Kim Saunders a missing person? Would it be over-reacting to ring the police? How stupid would Deb look though, if there was an ordinary explanation; Ray, the CareCorps boss, had said staying calm under pressure was essential in this job. And there was the immediate problem to deal with: Deb needed to send someone to Woodlands to cover Kim Saunders' shift tonight.

The door opened. 'Still no answer. You all right?'

Deb was staring again. 'Yes! I was just thinking... Maybe Kim's car wouldn't start on Saturday night. Someone might have given her a lift home.'

'But she'd have rung in, wouldn't she, if she couldn't get to work yesterday?'

'I suppose so. People don't always pass on messages.'

'You could be right,' said Rhoda. 'Shall I pop round to Kim's house after work, though, just to check if she's around?'

Surely that would make Deb look as though she was failing in her duty of care? 'No, don't worry. I can go at lunchtime; it's not far from here, is it? I'm meeting my sister, but she won't mind.'

'If you're sure, then,' said Rhoda.

'Oh and Rhoda,' Deb called out after her. 'Do keep ringing Kim, in case she is just ill.'

The house was semi-detached, with ageing paintwork; it reminded Deb of her own, although Kim's front garden wasn't covered in faded plastic toys. She rang the bell and heard it chime through the house. She tried again, waited, rapped on the door, then rang once more.

'No answer,' she told Hilary, who was in the passenger seat, sipping a take-away latte. She looked less care-worn since she had started her new job. Deb had a flashback to their childhood detective games, but kept it to herself. Reminders of her youthful foibles made Hilary tetchy. 'You're the detective, Hil. What do you think?'

'I think there's no one in.'

Deb elbowed her. 'No! I mean, what do I do? Should I raise the alarm or would I look ridiculous?'

'Well, there's not a lot to go on if you were thinking of reporting a missing person. You'd need friends and family saying, *She was meant to be here at this time and she didn't turn up.*'

'I've got no idea what her plans were. I know she has teenage kids, but I don't have any contact details for them.'

'So what's bothering you?'

'All that stuff about the clinic that Rhoda told me. It sounded so uncaring. And the boss, this uncle of Sarah's. Why would he dismiss good people for asking questions? I don't know. Maybe I'm just reading too much into it.'

Hilary gazed out of the windscreen and gave a shake of her head. 'Don't ignore your instincts. There's nothing airy-fairy about intuition, you know. Sometimes it's a primitive part of the brain telling you something's wrong. You know we do surveillance operations at the agency?' Deb was finding it hard to think straight and hoped she wasn't going off on a tangent. 'They're pretty high tech, but all legit and above board, because it has to be admissible in court. Anyway, we investigated that old people's home on the Ashbury Road. Some relatives were worried about the old people being neglected, but they didn't have any proof. So we sent in an investigator, posing as a care assistant. And she found awful stuff: bullying. Neglect. She got evidence, too. The court case is pending.'

'You mean we should send someone in to Woodlands?' Deb said, her mind lighting up with possibilities. What would Ray think of a surveillance operation? Even if Kim was OK, it might be worth pursuing because of the dismissals, which were costly to CareCorps and could damage its reputation. 'Would it be expensive?'

'Well, a quick look round by a very kind sister might not be.'

'Are you serious? Because if you are, I'll have to run it past Ray this afternoon. We need to send a replacement for tonight's shift.'

Hilary slurped the last of her coffee and wiped the foam from her lip. 'I'm serious,' she said.

CHAPTER THIRTY-THREE

38 weeks: Try to make the most of the last few days before the birth by enjoying yourself and getting as much rest as you can.

Sarah lay on the sofa on Monday afternoon, half willing herself to get sucked into the American talk show on TV. Her mobile beeped. It was a text from Helen at the office.

Hello lovely. How are you finding it at home?

Going quietly insane she replied. But then she added, *Daytime TV! Enough to drive anyone back to work.* Another beep brought the words: *Author here, speak later Xx,* and the phone went quiet.

A family on TV were flaunting how dysfunctional they were, trotting out shocking facts and then bellowing at each other. The studio audience roared in judgement – but Sarah's mind was too restless to engage.

What had Jim and her uncle really been talking about? Did they think she needed treatment for her mental state? Did Jim want the Gatehouse so much, he'd… *Oh God, stop it!* She was getting herself worked up again. No one was plotting anything. But then how paranoid, how mad were these thoughts?

Snatching up her mobile, she typed: *Hi Deb I...* then stopped, staring at the empty expanse after the words. What if Deb didn't reply? After a moment, she pressed 'delete'.

'Is that true?' The interviewer on TV was saying. 'Did you report her as an unfit mother?'

Sarah punched at the off button and tossed the remote away. It skidded across the coffee table and fell with a clatter to the floor. She reached for it, grabbing the legs of the statue on the phone table to steady herself. As she lifted her head, she found herself gazing at the pregnant figure.

The weight of the baby deep in her pelvis made her stop to catch her breath. She reached the top step and pushed open the attic door. The camping lantern hung on a hook inside, and she turned it on and held it at arm's length. The dust sheets had never been put back after her uncle's visit, and everything lay exposed to the murky glow. Clothes hung abandoned on rails; the wedding dress stood frozen in the shape of a woman. Sarah went over to one of the trunks, got awkwardly down on her knees and pushed back the lid.

Among the child's exercise books, school magazines and Brownie Handbooks, she found one or two things that must have belonged to a later Mary: a notebook with wobbly towers of accounts; a collecting book half-filled with Green Shield Stamps; and a guarantee for a Hoover, dated 1974. Her arm was tiring from holding up the lantern when she uncovered a narrow book with a fake leather cover, its corners decorated with gold-coloured trims. Flaking gold lettering said ADDRESSES. Inside were entries in backward-leaning handwriting. There was nothing under D for doctor, or S for Surgery. Sarah hauled herself to her feet, closed the trunk and sat on it to search the book from front to back.

There were details of the local school, a playgroup, a hairdresser and a coal merchant's. It did not seem much to show for an adult life. Sarah had got as far as R when she found 'Dr Rigby, Garden Street Surgery, Ashbury', and in Mary's sloping handwriting, a number.

The waiting room was packed and there was a huge queue for the reception desk. Taking her place at the end, Sarah leaned on a table piled with *Hello* magazines, while people in front of her organized prescriptions. The overheated air rang with coughing and babies crying. As the queue advanced, Sarah caught glimpses of the receptionist: a woman with thick, dry hair, speaking to people in clipped tones. Behind her, a kind-faced older woman in a nurse's uniform was looking through a filing cabinet.

At last, Sarah leaned forwards and spoke quietly to the

receptionist: 'I need to see my mother's medical records. She was a patient here with Dr Rigby until she died.'

'Records of deceased patients are sent to the County Health Authority. You'll have to apply to see them there.'

'Oh. You have nothing here at all?'

'How long ago did she die?'

'Twenty-six years.'

'Oh, no then. You're much too late.'

'What do you mean?' Sarah abandoned her quiet tone and the nurse looked up and caught her eye. The baby was pressing on her groin; she was starting to feel nauseous from standing, and there was a buzzing in her head.

'They destroy the records after ten years.'

'If you've finished, dear?' An elderly woman in an anorak pushed past Sarah with a poke of her elbow and slapped a prescription on the counter.

Sarah dragged her weight to a row of plastic chairs, and sank down onto one.

'Excuse me…' She opened her eyes to see a concerned face close to hers: it was the nurse. 'Are you all right?' Sarah did not trust herself to answer. 'What did you say your mother's name was?'

'Mary Greaves.'

'That's it! We were at school together! And I remember her bringing you here when you were little – with your brother. You're so much like her!' She put a hand over Sarah's. 'Look, why don't I have a look in the files, just to see if there's anything left.'

She bustled away and appeared moments later behind the desk, pulling out a drawer and flipping through files. Sarah pushed herself up and went to stand to one side of the queue.

'Well, what do you know!' the nurse said over the hubbub of enquiries, the crying of child. 'They are still here.'

'Can I see them?' said Sarah, but the nurse's smile faltered.

'Oh… I'm really sorry, but I'm not sure you can.'

'Why not?' cried Sarah. A woman in the queue turned to stare.

'I'm afraid there's no notification of death.'

'That means that rules of confidentiality still apply,' the

receptionist cut in with an air of triumph.

'What do I do now, then?'

'You have to bring in a death certificate,' said the receptionist. Sea noises sang in Sarah's ears. *Serve her bloody right if I have a stroke. Or give birth on their floor.* But then the nurse handed her a scrap of paper with a number on it.

Though darkness had fallen, there was no rush to get home; Jim had Lawsons' Christmas do and was staying the night at his Mum's. Sarah set off driving; she would ring from home. Then, stopping in a queue of traffic, she couldn't wait any longer and dialled the number. She listened to a complex series of options in a recorded voice, and punched at the keys as the traffic started to move again, driving with one hand.

By the time she was through to the right department, she had left the town behind and was on the open road that led through Tilden Cross. 'I need a copy of my mother's death certificate. Mary Greaves, née Briers.' She spelt out the names. 'I don't know the exact date, but it was September 1978. At Woodlands Clinic. Near Ashbury, yes.'

The line went quiet, apart from the clicking of a keyboard. She could see headlights coming from far away and thought that she would dip hers when the car got closer. The voice spoke again, but she could not make any sense of it. Suddenly lights were in her face and there was a screeching and blaring as a car swerved out of her way. Sarah hauled her steering wheel round and pushed her foot on the brake. The sudden halt juddered through her belly as she pressed the phone to her ear.

'What?' The other car had sped away and a hush fell on the deserted road, as if only Sarah and the phone voice existed.

'There is no death certificate in that name.'

CHAPTER THIRTY-FOUR

38 weeks: You will probably be feeling exhausted by now and you might just want to stay at home with your feet up.

A ghostly reflection of the lamp-lit living room partly obscured the darkness outside. Sarah's watch said almost ten. She turned the lamp off, then leaned her head against the glass, waiting for her eyes to adjust. Gradually, the garden emerged, and the woods beyond, heaving in the blustery night. Gently but definitely, her womb constricted.

She reached up to unlock the French windows. Jim might ring from his Mum's. It didn't matter; she had got beyond all that. The baby was due in a couple of weeks. She had to know. Outside, she pulled the door shut behind her without looking back.

The garden was an alien landscape in the dark. She felt her way down it, blundering once into a bush, and then fumbled for the ring to open the gate. Beyond the wall, she could see just enough to avoid bumping into trees, but brambles tore at her leggings and a branch she pushed sprang back and showered her with icy drops. She got into a waddling stride, feeling the weight of her body, but dragging it onwards. The tone and sound of the woods shifted from moment to moment: pale moonlight eased the blackness in snatches and the wind roared through the treetops, then fell quiet so that Sarah's own progress seemed cracklingly loud.

She kept on through the darkness, gasping with every step, until a branch thwacked her face and she clutched her cheek and swore. Her thighs ached and her hair was wet and wild, snagging on everything. Was this madness? She groped for something to lean on, and found that she had clutched a post of the chestnut paling that divided the Gatehouse land from Woodlands.

She couldn't stop now. Reaching up, she released her hair from a thorny mass and began to move along the fence, pushing at it. The first stretch felt firmly upright. She could not try to climb over it and risk a fall. Further along though, it seemed to sag; perhaps her uncle had never had it replaced after all. She started pushing harder, forcing the fence posts as far as they would go, and at last one leaned almost to the ground. She could crawl over here; her weight would flatten the fence beneath her.

She inched forwards on all fours, looking out for the rusted lacework of barbed wire, but then her hand slipped and spikes ripped into her wrist. She was almost over the fence, but the baby dragged her earthwards, and her leggings caught. She fought to disentangle herself, cursing through gritted teeth. Freed at last, she knelt in damp leaf debris, feeling for the first time the pain in her wrist. Pale moonlight revealed blood beading and then dripping from a gash.

The weight of her body felt like defeat; the earth beneath it was pungent with decay. She made herself look up, and some living thing – a fox? – took off running towards Woodlands. As Sarah turned to look after it, she saw lights.

The building was a shape in the blackness. Two lights shone in the tower, one above the other, but hardly any other windows were lit. Sarah emerged from the woods and shuffled as fast as she could manage across the lawn. A sign was lit by a discreet blue bar: ALL VISITORS MUST REPORT TO RECEPTION. She headed away from it, towards the cover of shadows.

Reaching a corner of the building, she stuck her head round. A young nurse leaned against the wall, smoking a cigarette. At Sarah's second peep, she was pushing the butt down a drain with her toe. Head down, arms tight across her chest, she turned and went inside.

After an interval, Sarah crept up to the door. It was still ajar. The room looked like an old back kitchen, with a big square sink, but now spades and garden shears poked out of the dimness, and along a wide shelf was a mess of pots, trowels and twine.

She clenched her fists in victory as she stepped inside. Feeling her way through a stale waft of cigarette smoke, she found the other door, which opened onto a neon-lit corridor. No one was about.

Back in the store, she raked her fingers through her hair and hauled off her muddy coat. She should try to look like a doctor or a social worker with a reason to be here. This was a big place; they might not look twice at a newcomer. She wiped her hands on the clean, wet parts of the coat, then passed them over her face. Her scarf doubled as a towel, which she then stuffed under her coat. She pushed both to the back of a shelf.

Stepping outside, she began to move along the corridor, close to the wall.

A door opened and women's voices sounded. Sarah began to move faster. The voices were coming closer. She saw steps leading down to a door and found herself rushing towards them and stepping downwards.

On the other side of the door, the corridor was quiet and still. Sarah stood recovering from her jolting descent, thinking she would wait and let the voices pass. But they seemed to get closer; was it possible they were coming down too? They'd know that she had no business down here! She moved along the stark space, came to a door and opened it. Tables and chairs were stored inside in unsteady-looking piles. There was a thump and the sound of footsteps; two sets at least. Sarah stepped quickly inside and shut the door. The footsteps advanced, sounded outside the door and passed on – but then seemed to pause. She should stay in here a moment longer to be sure.

'I don't know where her key's got to,' said a woman's voice. 'I'm just going to get you one from the orderlies' sets – they're down here.'

'Thank you.' Another voice, oddly familiar. 'And did you say the tower's in the other wing?'

'Yeah. I'll show you on the way back.'

Sarah pushed open the door and looked down the corridor. Two nurses were turning a corner out of view. She stepped out and hurried after them, pursuing the receding voices.

John leaned back in his chair in the tower study with the black folder open on his knees. With his eyes locked on a picture, he willed himself to be lifted above all these simmering issues that threatened to come to a head. The nurse had fought with such terrified strength – the memory mingled with the appeal of the picture... 'Think, John!' said an inner voice. Like Father, barracking him on through his schoolwork in this very room. He had broken off once and stared through rising cigarette smoke at the woods. 'Women don't think, John. They don't analyse; they don't plan. That's why you and I will always get the better of them. Now, get back to work. She mollycoddled you, but she's gone. We're going to make something of you.'

Think. He had done nothing else since Saturday. He had hardly slept. The last text sent from the nurse's phone said, *Have a lovely time at Dad's. See you Weds eve XX.* It was only Monday night; he could sort things out by then, surely – he just had to think tactically. But chill thoughts flashed: the blood spatters when the little fire extinguisher knocked into her skull; his damn pager beeping when he was going through her pockets, before he could even check that she was dead. His erection faltered and sank.

He had kept his head, hadn't he? The pager could end up being his alibi, so he had washed in the anteroom sink, sprinted from the basement room then hurried over to the East Wing and hurled the black folder in the tower study. He was with Orr-Hughes, dealing with his stupid admission query within five minutes at most – as if he had been in his office all along.

Sunday and today had passed in furtive, frustrated action. He had incinerated the clothes he had been wearing, and made preparations with syringes and capsules in case the worst came to the worst. Saunders' car was still in the car park and he would have to remove it. Its keys must be in the locker room. He had walked past it several times with her locker and room keys in his pocket but there were always people in the corridor. He could hardly pop his head round the door.

On top of that, the bloody chaplain was showing round do-gooders from the local church. John had tried to get to the basement corridor a couple of times, but had had to turn back. He must go tonight and check; she was surely dead now if not before. Would the body burn in their small incinerator? Would the bones remain? The car would give away the fact that she was still here. But what if he dragged the corpse into the woods and left it there? Then some patient might have done it – he thought of big, strong-looking ones with a history of violence. Nothing would implicate him. He would remove all signs of his plans from the new treatment room in the basement.

But he had been a new man, making those plans; that chat with Jim had sparked such a blaze of hope. Was it all being snatched away because of that interfering bitch? She had ruined everything. He was glad that he had killed her. He was aroused again, and focused hard on the picture, imagining giving both of them the punishment they deserved. But oh God, it was all such an effort. He was so very tired.

'It's through there,' the staff nurse said, nodding towards an unpainted, unmarked door. 'There's just the one patient and the boss's private office.' Sarah's watch said eleven-fifteen. She had followed them through exhausting miles of corridor, keeping out of sight, as the staff nurse showed the newcomer from the agency round. She was now pressed against the wall around the corner from where they stood. 'Right, I'll show you to the nurse's station and leave you to it,' the staff nurse said.

The swing doors thudded and Sarah looked round the corner to find them gone. She crossed to the door and went inside. She was at the bottom of a dimly lit, winding staircase. Her hand pressed cold, pitted plaster as she began to climb, trying to keep her footsteps silent. She heaved herself up steps and more dizzying steps, until one more turn revealed a door. The private office or the patient's room? She saw a tarnished brass sign – *John Briers* – and hurried on upwards, picturing the door opening, his eyes on her back.

Her legs were trembling. Her foot slipped with a scuffing sound and she gasped – then round the next turn was another door. As she reached the threshold, the baby squirmed inside her. She took hold of the handle and turned.

It wouldn't open. She was stunned for a moment and then realised that it was locked. But then – did she hear something? She pressed her ear to the door. Were those sounds of movement, or her own breathing, her bloodstream's roar? She held her breath and the sounds stopped. She put her lips to the door and whispered: 'Hello?' Silence. 'Hello? It's Sarah.'

There was a shuffling, but again it fell quiet. Had a stranger got back into bed, not knowing who Sarah was? She heard a whispery dragging, coming closer. Someone was breathing on the other side of the door. Then a scrape and a click, and the handle moved.

CHAPTER THIRTY-FIVE

38 weeks: Make sure you always have your birth partner's contact details on you. These days, many women choose a good friend or their own mother to help them through the delivery.

It was the apparition from the night-time garden. Sarah let out a cry. Now she was being dragged inside. She shrank back against the door. Blue eyes fixed on her. A greyed nightdress hung on prominent bones. As the wild-haired woman moved closer, she reached out a hand. Sarah screamed.

The hand went over her mouth. The woman pressed a finger to her own lips; her face contorted. She took her hand from Sarah's mouth and pointed a shaking finger towards the stairs. Her face began to work with a twitching motion. A hiss emerged and, with a grunt of strain, turned into a whisper.

'Sss-Sarah! It's mm-ee!'

Sarah hunched over and ducked her head, clutching at her temples. Mad hair tickled her face. Time slowed down. Then she breathed in a trace of something ancient and lost: all the world's comfort in the scent of warm skin.

Something ruptured in her chest and throat, releasing a tide. Tears spilled over and ran from her chin. She slumped forwards, her neck wet.

Her mother took her arms and led her. Her legs touched a bed – she was sitting on it. When she managed to lift her head, her mother sat staring at her with fearful tenderness. There was a story in that look, a story different from her uncle's.

Awareness of the here and now snatched hold of Sarah. He might be downstairs. 'They told us you were dead,' she said.

Mary pressed a hand to her throat. The voice that came was hoarse, but stronger. 'John locked me up here.'

Because of what you did. 'He said you tried to kill me.'

Mary looked down at her hands. She wasn't denying it, then? Sarah struggled to stand. Her mother reached out to her, a desperate appeal in her eyes. Her voice rasped in snatches. 'He's used me – since we were children. He's made me have sex with him. Forced me.' Sarah's legs had no strength; her weight pulled her down on to the bed. 'I thought it would stop when I got married. But… It didn't. And then I found him – trying to get to you.' The hand that took Sarah's was shaking. 'I couldn't go on. I knew David would be OK with Michael – but you needed me. I couldn't leave you...' Sarah snatched her hand away. 'I thought it would be peaceful … painless, with a pillow. I had pills for me in my pocket. But you woke up. And David screamed…'

Sarah's body clenched like a fist.

'I'm so sorry... I meant us to be safe, away from him. But I did a terrible thing. I know that.'

Poor thing. Monster. Sarah's heart swung in confusion. Where would it end? She was looking at herself from outside. She saw herself reach out and take the thin, dry hand in hers.

There was a long moment of stillness. Then her mother spoke again. 'Can I ask you ... about David?'

Sarah managed a whisper. 'He's OK.'

'Poor boy. He was so wary of me, near the end. I had to shoo him away when John came. I'd hear him scuttling in hallways. *Little mouse,* I called him.'

A sharp knock sounded in the tower and Mary leapt to her feet. 'You must go! Get away from him!'

'He can't keep you here like this!' Sarah said, but Mary pulled her towards the door.

'Doesn't matter about me. You get away. I came – I tried to warn you. I look over the woods every day and I think of you. It's all I want. You safe. And your baby.'

Sarah's mind raced. 'I need to ask you – did your mother go mad? He said it was in the family.'

Mary's head twitched towards the door and back. 'Mad? No. She got pregnant with another man. She left us to be with him.' She put both hands to Sarah's face. 'Please – he's coming. You must go.'

Sarah found herself pushed; she was out on the landing. 'I'll come back for you.'

'Sarah, my lovely. Just get away.'

The landing felt cold with the door closed between them. There were sounds from below again. Sarah began to step too quickly down the stairs. She saw his door, and almost retreated. But she made herself move on. Right outside it, she stumbled and slapped a steadying hand on the wall.

John stirred, asleep in his chair in the tower study and sucked in a stream of drool. Excitement sickened and waned; an awful awareness rising. He was dream-walking down the basement corridor to the new treatment room. He was going to have to cut up the nurse's body and post it to his mother. His father insisted. He had brown paper for the parcel ready in his hand. What would have become of the body since the sick crunch of death? But when the door opened with a clatter, the chair with the straps was empty.

There was another sound above, but Sarah kept going, thudding on step after step. She reached the door at the bottom, and grasped at nothing in the dimness. At last she found the handle and burst into electric brightness.

CHAPTER THIRTY-SIX

38 weeks: Since you don't know when labour will start, keep in touch with your nearest and dearest at all times. Enjoy this time as a couple before the new arrival.

Dazzling. An explosion of light behind her eyes. Then twinkling, bursting points. No pain, just silence, then soft darkness. Fading. Bursting back; neck hurting, legs, arms. Cough jolting everything. Head cold. Wet.

Red in the dimness, and porridge. Sickness, fading. Coming back into focus – red; porridge. Mind struggling, swimming up. Ah! The smell. Not porridge. Vomit. Back of head ragged, chilled. Hanging forwards, tightness on legs and arms, neck aching. Why? Don't fade. Kick upwards. Him. Pictures. Jane. He was strapping her arms down. Kim beat, bashed, fought. His strength, shocking. She saw Tom and Amy growing up without her. He was in the dark behind her. Crunch. Fireworks. Now this. Hours passed, hanging, nauseous, staring at vomit. Sitting in wetness; she had let go in terror. Now great snotty sobs, making the pain worse. No one came down here, and she couldn't move or cry out. The floor dark and sticky with her blood. She could still hear it dripping. *God why? How could you? Where are you?* She had come down here to help someone, a prayer on her lips. Only exhaustion stopped her crying. She hung in the dark that came, wakeful but spent.

Would he come back to finish her off? Throbbing seared the back of her head, and straps tore her skin, blocking the blood flow to her limbs. She hung, obsessed by thirst, neck unbearable, shivering, cold. He might as well put her out of her misery.

No. She would not let him kill her. What had that bastard done to Jane, and now her? They couldn't let him beat them.

Could she survive? Head injury risks: bleeding, tearing and swelling of the brain. In a closed injury, bleeding had nowhere to go; it pressed on brain tissue and could damage critical areas. Think it through. Her head was just pain now. Before, it felt crumpled and cold. He must have smashed her skull. She swallowed dry foulness and retched. An open injury let the pressure out. But there was the risk of infection and bleeding. *Don't get confused; don't fall into a coma.*

Oh, how desperate she was for a drink. Think it through, then. Tea time at the nurse's station. Who would be on shift? Terri, Ayanna, Chris – and Inger! Kim would miss the party for her 50th. And coffee with Graham. He would think she'd stood him up. Think through the tea round: Terri's hippy herbal things; Ayanna: strong with a dash of milk; Inger: builder's with two sugars; Chris: coffee with Sweetex. She imagined the process, would not let herself miss anything: the papery pyramid teabag, the orange light on the kettle, the little plastic pedal clicking off, steam everywhere, head back – her mascara wasn't waterproof. Sloshing hot liquid in the mugs – not right to the dregs or you get the white bits of scale. Brown seeping out, swirling. Waiting. Milk to mix the precise colour, warm orange-brown; then fishing out the teabag, plopping it steaming in the bin. Only then would she picture the taste of her own cup: hot, wet, reviving, the perfect balance of earthy, metallic tea and the cool blandness of milk. Oh God, the world's best drink. In her head she drank it in. She would not let him kill her.

Sarah hardly knew how she got back to the Gatehouse. It was only when she stepped inside, snapped on the lamp and bolted the French windows that she felt the demon at her back turning away. *She got pregnant with another man, and left us to be with him.* She stood, her head swimming with exhaustion, her body hurting in places she couldn't even name. But in the midst of it, calm was descending. Sleep was coming to engulf her. As she collapsed on to the sofa, her womb squeezed tight and hard, and found her heart at peace.

Dim light. Tea, nurses. Who on duty now? Neck and back wracked tight. Head aching. Hands, feet, numb. Chilled to the bone, corpse-cold. Tea. Iyanna. Who had what? She must concentrate, but it wouldn't follow, it was slipping away. Paul telling Tom and Amy: *I'm so sorry, Mum's dead.* No, keep going! If she screwed up the strength, could she cry out? She uttered a little gasp; but even she could hardly hear it. Dead meat, hanging there, voiceless. *Oh God, please help me. Don't let this be it.*

'Help me. Hemme.' A pathetic noise. Faint and fading.

It was well into the morning when Sarah woke up, aching and sore. As soon as she surfaced, she thought of the baby with a surge of warm brightness. She had not been excited; it had all been stifled. She wanted Jim there to show him: she was excited now.

She stood up from the sofa, amazed that she had slept there, and made herself a cup of tea, standing in yesterday's dirty clothes. She was supposed to have cut out caffeine, but the urge for tea was overwhelming. She put toast on, but when she went to get butter, there was a wedge of cheesecake at eye height in the fridge. She stood at the open door eating it while her toast popped up and went cold.

Washing up the cheesecake plate, she thought of her mother in the tower room, and her hands fell still in the water. The sky over the woods had patches of blue with ragged cloud hurrying over it. Jim would be home soon, for a shower before a late morning appointment. She would tell him the good news. But she must call David first. She imagined him exclaiming – would he be delighted or shocked? Perhaps she should tell him in person.

'Sarah, this is ridiculous,' David said. 'What have you done? Talked to some bloody mental patient and persuaded her she's our dead mother...'

He had insisted she told him on the phone. Now he was here, she kept having to repeat herself. 'David, I told you, there's no death certificate. I mean – did you go to a funeral? Visit a grave? No, because they locked her up at Woodlands and lied to us. She's in that tower now, completely at his mercy. We've got to get her out of there.'

'I can't believe I'm listening to this. I'm supposed to pick Joe up from nursery.' He looked up. She could hear a car – or more than one? Doors slammed.

A familiar voice: 'Mr Mercer?'

A key crunched, the front door opened, and a moment later Jim came in, looking harried. Over his shoulder, Sarah saw Ralph Farnham. Her doctor.

'Sarah?' Jim dropped his bag and came towards her, but then stopped where David stood.

'Are you all right? What's going on?'

'I'm just talking to David. I've got good news, Jim, but – who called the doctor?'

'David was worried about you.'

She tried to steady her voice. 'I found out that there was no death certificate for my mother. I went over to Woodlands and I found her. She's alive. I've talked to her. Uncle John locked her up there. He's abused her for years.'

'Sarah, what have you been doing? Your mother's dead.'

'Jim! Go there with the police. You'll see.'

'Do you mind if I just check..?' Doctor Farnham had a blood pressure cuff. Jim stood aside and he sat down beside Sarah. Jim and David stood watching. She imagined pummelling their chests with her fists; the doctor dragging her away. A tentative hand pushed up her sleeve. There on her wrist was the gash from the barbed wire, now a jagged line of dark dried blood.

Jim drew in his breath. 'What've you done?!'

'We'll need to clean that up.' Dr Farnham put on the cuff and began pumping it up.

'I did it on some barbed wire going through the woods. I'm all right. Jim, really – I'm fine. It's all going to be okay, with the baby. There's nothing wrong with me.' Blood surged in her ears and her vision swam. She wasn't all right; she didn't feel right at all.

'Mrs Mercer,' the doctor said. 'I think we should get you into hospital for some rest.' What did he mean? She looked at Jim; his eyes were shining. 'I'm concerned about your blood pressure. I think we should admit you to the maternity unit early, so we can keep an eye on things.'

Her blood pressure. It must be through the roof; that's why she felt so strange. She covered her face and felt hot breath on her palms.

'Sarah, please. To be safe.' Jim's voice was tight.

'All right. All right. But – I need to have a shower and pack my things.'

'Of course,' the doctor said. 'I'll see if they can admit you this afternoon.'

There were sighing and shuffling noises and when she looked, Jim was seeing the doctor out. It seemed very quiet in the room, though she heard muttering in the hallway. David put his hands together with an infuriating clap as though he was getting a grip on things. He went to speak but she blurted out, 'You can't face it, can you? You're on the bloody run from everything. No wonder she called you *Little Mouse.*' She heaved herself up from the sofa and stood still until the floor stopped see-sawing. Then she pushed past him and went to have her shower.

CHAPTER THIRTY-SEVEN

38 weeks: You will need your partner's support more than ever. He can help you to feel confident, safe and relaxed as the birth approaches.

Everyone told Hilary she had an innocent face; it was an asset in this business as it had been in the police. If she put on a chirpy voice, people assumed she was naïve and unthreatening. Mel, the nurse who had briefed her at the start of the shift, had probably confided more than she normally would to the wide-eyed new 'agency nurse'. Then again, perhaps she actually thought this place had nothing to hide. She had described the patients to Hilary in terms of whether or not they would 'give you any trouble'. A pale, thin man in the West Wing had got agitated earlier, repeating over and over, 'Where is the kind nurse? She said she would come back.'

'Looks like she's stood you up, then,' Mel had replied.

'But we were going to have a chat. She said she wouldn't be long.'

Mel had leaned over and shouted in his face: 'You'd better stop that broken record right now. Because no one wants to hear it!'

Hilary passed a window as she hurried along a corridor. A night of fitful rain had turned into a bright morning; an unwelcome sight when you have had no sleep. There was a lot to fit in before her shift ended. She had found Kim's car in the staff car park, from Rhoda's description of the Yaris model and the unusual aubergine colour. Copper-coloured leaves were gathering on its windscreen. She still wanted to check for Kim's bag. Mel had mentioned a party later; perhaps that would get some of the staff out of the way for a while. She saw Chris, a stocky male nurse, approaching.

'Nurse's station on West Wing B!' he called. 'Quick gathering for Inger's 50th before we knock off.'

'Oh right. Thanks! Why don't I keep an eye on things while you lot go? I don't mind, honestly.'

'Suit yourself,' he said, walking backwards with a smile. 'But come if you change your mind. There's cake!'

Hilary reached the corridor outside the West Wing nurses' locker room and found it deserted. Slipping inside, she pushed a bin against the door to delay anyone coming in. If discovered, she'd say she was stupidly shy of people walking in when she was changing. She even practised a rueful grin and unbuttoned the top of her uniform to complete the effect.

She took the professional pick and tension wrench from her pocket. Mel had muttered earlier, when allocating her locker, 'Kim's is locked. Someone else must have nabbed it.' Hilary had noted the locker: number 47. She went over to it now and pushed the tension wrench into the lower part of the keyhole. Luckily, since she had her own locker, she knew which way to turn, and she gently turned clockwise and held the wrench in place. Careful to shield the locker with her crouching body, she put the pick in the upper part of the lock and pressed up. She could feel the pins resisting her pressure, and jiggled expertly, trying to find which pair was the hardest to push up. Eventually she thought she had identified the toughest ones, and pushed up until she heard a faint click: the upper pin falling down on top of the cylinder, out of the way. Good. The lower pin was not resisting much now, and moved up a fraction when she pressed it. She moved on to the other pins, listening out for movement in the corridor. Once the cake was eaten and the shift ended, they would all head straight back here.

Her thighs ached from squatting. She heard footsteps and leaned to conceal the locker, reluctant to let go of the tension wrench, which would mean having to start all over again. The steps plodded closer, hesitated for a horrible moment, and then went lumpily past. Hilary breathed again. She kept on applying torque and pushing up pins, her calves threatening to cramp and cold creeping down the open front of her uniform. At last, all the pins were pushed up out of the way, and she turned the tension wrench, willing the cylinder to be released. It resisted. She jiggled the wrench and tried again. The cylinder turned and the locker opened.

Inside was a brightly coloured bag in ethnic fabric. Keeping her left hand on the tools in the lock, Hilary pulled the bag onto her lap and rifled through it. A label inside said, *Made by South Indian women rescued from the sex trade.* There was a folding umbrella, keys on a Toyota fob, a crumpled church newsletter and a blueberry cereal bar. Weighing down the bottom was a bulky purse. Hilary opened the wallet part and saw a driving licence and bank cards: *Kim Saunders.* She whipped a miniature camera from her pocket and pressed the button with one hand. When she had put everything back in the bag, she saw a gift-wrapped parcel at the back of the locker. A taped-on envelope said, *Inger* with a wiggly flourish.

The woman who bought that bag, penned that flourish had probably never left the building. Hilary's chest clenched. She shoved everything in the locker, shut the door and jiggled at the lock until it clicked back into place. Pocketing her tools, she stood up on numb, unsteady legs.

She would have to get the police involved. She buttoned up her uniform, dragged the bin aside and began walking towards the East Wing. The thought of the tower nagged at her – she'd have to get there before she left. Briers had an office up there, and there was a patient, behind a locked door, who was his sole responsibility. Mel gave the place a wide berth, because it 'gave her the creeps'. But Kim Saunders was always up there. Hilary was doing Kim's rounds, so the tower was what Amal would call a *legitimate target*. She reached the heavy wooden door Mel had shown her and stepped inside.

She began to climb carefully up the stairs, but almost immediately heard movement above and retreated to the bottom. There was a noise like a doorknob rattling, and heavy footsteps.

'Mary?'

She pulled back into the shadows. More footsteps. A door closed. Hilary felt a great headrush of adrenaline. She ran softly up the stairs and found a door marked *John Briers*. It stood ajar.

Jim had been having breakfast at Mum's, being fussed over like a boy on a school day, but with a man-sized hangover. Then David had called with Sarah's ridiculous claims. He had sounded aggressive, as if Jim were responsible and should sort it out. Jim had said, 'Fuck,' out loud; had seen Mum's face fall. He had made some excuse about a problem at work, and called David back from the car. That's when they decided to get the doctor out. Why would she start up about her mother again? Jim had tried so hard to put that awful night down to a nightmare, but on the drive home, he had thought of all those articles about motherhood and madness.

He dropped down onto the living room sofa. 'She's asleep. She kept telling me to go over there with the police.' David seemed rooted to the spot, staring ahead. His face had a strange grey sheen. 'I think she's having some kind of breakdown,' Jim said. David still didn't answer. 'What?' Jim said.

David went to speak, croaked and started again. 'Maybe we should go over there.'

'What do you mean? Why?'

David had one elbow in the air as if he were trying to hold a wall up; his fist was stuck in his hair.

'Sarah said something Mum used to say… She called me *Little Mouse*,'cos I was nervous. But it was just between us. Sarah couldn't have known... Unless she'd seen her.'

A domino run was set off inside Jim's head. Things he had been sure of came thunking down, one after the other, and smashed to pieces.

'You think she's really seen her?'

David made a scoffing sound, as though he found that laughable. But then he said, 'I can't see how else...'

'Shit, David. Shit! I've been treating her like a lunatic!'

He had gone into the bathroom when she was in the shower. She had turned to him, dripping, absurdly pregnant, and her face was desolate, crying.

'You're going to find out it's all true,' she had said. 'I just wish you'd believe it from me.'

Oh Christ, why hadn't he believed her? He was so out of his depth. That offer from her uncle had been terrible – but tempting. He leapt to his feet. 'What did Sarah say? About your Mum and that?'

'That she found her in the tower. She said Uncle John abused her and then locked her up there all this time. And lied about there being madness in the family.'

Uncle Fucking John. The months since Sarah had met him swept past Jim in a high-speed display: the stories, the upsets; the terror. Did he have the mother in his clutches? If he did, then he'd been stringing Sarah along, feeding her lies… Shit, was he after her too? He must be! And Jim had been no use to her. He had been so cocksure he was doing the right thing, but he had failed her. 'Shit. Dave. We've got to get over there. C'mon,' he said. 'Come on!'

'Ok,' David said, but he was still just standing there. And they couldn't leave Sarah, could they? But Jim had to do this for her at least; he had to.

'Can you ring Deb?' he said. 'Ask her to come over and stay with Sarah?'

'She's at work. I'm meant to pick Joe up…'

'Dave, please!'

David struggled to use his mobile, blinking and shielding his eyes; then he spoke in staccato phrases in a tight voice, and only half explained. Jim overheard Deb's response: 'David, what's going on? Why are you with Sarah? After all we've said!'

'Just come, Deb, please,' David said.

John's shadow lay across the floor between them, but Mary knew not to raise her head. Her hand still felt warm from her daughter's touch. She had a stupid urge to shout and laugh. Might she see David again as well? John mustn't see the quiver that went through her at the thought. But then he shifted and his shadow crossed her feet. The hope sank away, ridiculous.

'What's got into you? You know you can't keep things from me!' His voice was jolly, with an edge of ice. She should steel herself, but her mind skittered about, as if Sarah had blown a hole in the grim life of the tower and the light was pouring in.

She had managed to warn her – she'd get away, wouldn't she? Mary pictured her throwing a suitcase in the boot of a car, and before she could stop it, her gaze rose from the floor and looked out over the woods. She looked down again quickly, but she'd seen his pupils, big and black.

'You've seen her!' Her insides shrank. 'She's been here! Hasn't she?'

He can't keep you here like this! No one had ever said that her imprisonment here was wrong. But it was. She jerked her head up and looked him full in the face.

She saw his startled look, then an odd, twisted smile starting – but she did not see his hand coming. She flew back, felt the crack of the wall on the back of her head, and tasted blood. Then he was on her, her hair in his fists, his face an inch from hers.

'You mad bitch! What have you done?'

Time hung still. He let go of her and the soles of her feet thudded onto lino: he had lifted her up off the floor. Her scalp was ripped; she felt the imprint of his knuckles in her skull. Flushed purple, he leaned into her face.

'What did you think she'd do? Invite you home? Take you away from me?!' His laugh was a hacking sound. 'Sarah knows what you are. You're the so-called mother who tried to murder her, in her nursery. In her little bed!' His eyes flitted about. 'She'll go to the police. I kept you out of prison, Mary! Now you'll be locked up, without me. For anyone to get their hands on. No. No. She'll have to go.'

Mary's whole frame trembled as if she would shake herself apart.

His hands moved to her face, still raw from the slap, then went around her, pulling her close. 'They won't take you away from me. I won't be without you.' She gasped to catch her breath in his straitjacket hug. *But he can't get to Sarah while he's doing this.*

She felt hot breath in her ear and heard him whisper: 'Maybe there is a way... for us to be together. Neither of us left behind, alone.' He reached into his jacket pocket and lifted something out, then grasped her hair and twisted her head round. Between his finger and thumb was a transparent tub, and in it, two big capsules. Some new medication? The hand in her hair was stroking her with a dreamy gentleness. 'One for each of us.' Mary fell off the edge and plummeted through space, but she landed with a jolt in the same nightmare.

There were muffled shouts and thuds from above that took Hilary straight back to police operations. Should she go up and intervene? No, if he was dangerous, she would be of no use alone; and she must snatch this opportunity while she could. A black leather doctor's bag was on the floor beside the desk. She snapped the clasp and opened it to reveal a jumble of plastic pill tubs and vials and an unopened pack of syringes. She picked out two tubs: *Haloperidol*, *Lorazepam*. She repeated the names to herself, then dropped them back in the bag. The desk was old and battered and the central drawer stuck before jolting open. There were post-it notes, years' worth of appointment diaries, staples and elastic bands. Hilary fanned through the pages of the diaries, but only conferences and meetings were scrawled inside. She jiggled the drawer shut.

It seemed quieter upstairs. A good sign? Or not? She dragged out folders from the back of the desk and flipped through them. Accounts, staff lists, rotas – all a few years old. She heard creaking and thought of the lack of hiding places in here; if he came back, she'd have to rush behind the door, like a character in a farce.

No time to check the ancient computer – it would take ages to boot up. A black folder, like those on the desk, lay on the chair, and she grabbed and opened it, thinking what her next move should be. Rows of images on A4 pages in plastic file sheets. Hilary's police-brain said, *Got him.* She saw the place raided, Briers' head pushed through the doorway of a patrol car, a proper search for Kim Saunders behind fluttering police tape. At the very least, they'd have him for sexual and physical abuse, over years. But how grim the prize was. She was staring at things most people never have to see: the close-up shame of a woman with an erection forced in her mouth; a frail-looking hospital patient in poses from violent porn. Hilary shut the file but the pictures were still there behind her eyelids.

Jim's resolve mounted as they stepped out in the December cold and headed for the car. They bumped through the woods and sped along the country roads to Woodlands' main entrance. He ignored the 'Slow, max 5mph' signs on the driveway and the wheels spat gravel in all directions. He parked haphazardly in a reserved bay.

They stormed into the reception area with its leather sofas and potted ornamental trees. Jim recognised the young receptionist. She smiled so nicely from her circular island that you could almost believe that he and David were bursting into this tranquil place in the grip of a shared delusion.

'We need to see John Briers,' he said.

'Do you have an appointment?'

'No.'

The girl's smile faded. She made a quick gesture of tucking a lock of hair over her ear, though every strand was captured in a ponytail. 'I'm afraid you can't see him without an appointment.'

'We need to speak to him now.' Jim's own voice sounded blunt and rough; the Kentish boy in him unleashed by the crisis. 'It's important. You need to call him...'

'No, I'm afraid I can't.'

Surely David would enter the bloody fray at some point? But he was pushing a hand to his brow, and shrugged when Jim caught his eye.

'I wish I'd kept my bloody mouth shut,' he said.

Jim leaned over the reception desk, his posture a barely veiled threat. 'John Briers is my wife's uncle. We need to talk to him urgently and we want to see him now.'

The receptionist looked as if her lip might start to tremble.

Saliva flooded Mary's mouth as she pressed the capsule upwards with her tongue.

'You've given me no other choice,' he said. 'It's either this, or she has to go.' He lay propped beside her on one elbow, watching. She saw the parchment colour of him, his eyes manic one minute, tender the next. Was this how it ended? Or could she wait and spit and defeat him at last? She thought his eyes filled with tears as he slapped his own capsule to his mouth, then he closed them and grimaced as he gulped it down.

Lie down, lose consciousness – die! But he just gazed at her. 'We've been everything to each other. Entwined lives. Twin deaths. It makes perfect sense.'

Wouldn't he ever stop watching her? Her mouth frothed around the foreign object; the gelatine coating of the capsule slackened, slick and fragile against her tongue. It was like some childhood game of who blinks first, gone horribly wrong. And now the capsule collapsed in on itself and a bitter rush of powder seeped into her mouth. She struggled to sit up, but his arm clamped over her, and she turned and saw his gritted teeth and wetness on his cheeks.

Mary tasted the acrid tang of poison. She would never see David again, or hold Sarah's baby. But John was dying with her. Sarah would be safe. Her throat convulsed and her tongue let go. The capsule and its vile spillage slipped down.

She felt a choking burn. There was a terrible wrongness and nausea and the need to struggle; she thought her body might vomit the capsule and expel the poison. But then a golden calm warmed though her, and lifted her away on its tide. She could do this last thing for Sarah. She wanted nothing more now. She prayed, 'Thank you! Thank you!' as everything fell away.

For a time she was suspended in peacefulness, quietly fading. Then through the dark woods she saw a light shining, and knew that all would be well. With all her dark fears behind her, she ran towards home.

Sarah jolted awake, her insides gripped by a huge constricting pain. She had been dreaming that she was a little girl and David was sitting on her stomach, telling her it was a game and he was winning. 'David, get off, it really hurts!' she had shouted. Staring at the beamed ceiling, she realised that the pains had been going on for some time. And this one was taking her over.

When he felt Mary relax under his tight restraining arm, John finally let himself lie down. Exhaustion engulfed him and carried him with it. He felt for Mary's hand and held it. No one could separate them now. He could still not believe it had come to this. And not even because of the nurse, but because Sarah had found out about Mary. He knew how the outside world would see his arrangements; they would destroy him. But the world's view of right and wrong was a great phoney facade; it had never made sense in their lives. He thought of their nursery days: him and Mary, huddled together for comfort.

Somewhere below, a phone began to ring.

His eyes sprang open. He turned to look at Mary. Her mouth gaped, and the skin hung slackly from her bones. A tear track snaked from her eye down into her hair. He could tell straight away that she was dead. He laid her hand down beside her body, but the phone pierced through the gesture, ringing on and on. Couldn't people leave them alone? *But I am alone; I am alone now.* He had a sudden picture of Sarah with her hand on that disgusting belly.

He sat up and opened his fist. The capsule was stuck to his palm. It trembled and glistened in the light from the window. He stared at it, then dropped it in his pocket.

Shit, the phone, the noisy bloody phone. He'd hear it, surely, and come back down. Hilary tipped the plastic casing up with one hand, looking for the ringer button to turn it off, but just then Deb's voice sounded in the mobile pressed to her ear. 'Hilary? What's going on?'

'I've found Kim Saunders's car and bag. I don't think she ever left. And Briers has pictures of sexual abuse and violence, probably against a patient. He's dangerous, Deb. I'm going to hand this over to the police.'

Over Deb's exclamation, Hilary heard a door being opened upstairs. She whirled round and rushed behind the door, her back pressed to the wall. Footsteps came nearer and nearer. She strained to listen, then jumped, as Deb's voice from the mobile said, 'Hilary?' There was a double thud and a scuffing; two feet stepping heavily on to the landing. The door swung towards her and came to rest on the tips of her shoes. Beyond its edge, she caught a flash of tweed. Something was being dragged across the floor. The door swung away again and the footsteps sounded, going down.

'Sorry,' she whispered into her mobile, 'I'm still here.' The office phone stopped ringing at last, its echo reverberating through the sudden quiet. The footsteps became fainter and a door was closed below. 'I just need to check something,' Hilary said, reluctant to break off the call. The doctor's bag had gone. She went out onto the landing and began to walk upwards on shaking legs.

Hilary found the patient's room and fished in her pocket for the key. Her hand shook a little as she unlocked and pushed open the door. She saw a woman lying on her back on the bed, and crept closer. A purple hand-print bruise spread over one side of her face, and blood showed at the edges of her lips. It was the woman from the photographs. Her eyes were half open. Hilary recognised the glassy stare of death.

'I'm going to ring the police,' Hilary said. She made herself scan the crime scene. Then a movement in the window caught her eye. A figure in a tweed jacket was striding across the lawn, towards the woods.

'Deb!' she said. 'Briers is heading for the Gatehouse.'

CHAPTER THIRTY-EIGHT

38 weeks: It is normal to feel anxious about the delivery, but remember it is very rare for anything to go wrong.

A grip of iron grabbed Sarah's womb. She leaned over the phone table and grasped the statue, her fingers joining round its legs. She must do her breathing, but couldn't think straight. Where was Jim? A vague memory from half-sleep said he had gone out. Her mobile was nowhere around; she picked up the house phone. A wave of pressure overtook her, like a period pain but tighter, fiercely pulling at her core.

'Sarah?'

'Jim, come back, I'm having contractions. I think it's starting. Where are you?'

'Oh God, really? Is Deb there?'

'What? No. Just come back, please.'

'I'm coming. And Sarah... I'm sorry. Don't worry.'

'Okay,' she said, 'okay.'

She hung up. The squeezing ache subsided and faded, leaving a sudden peace. She wanted to move and straightened up, trying to remember what she was meant to do. What stage was she at anyway? How long since the pains started, when she was asleep? She walked back and forth, then over to the sofa and beyond, but already another heaving ache was building. Jim was meant to time all this. He had shown her the gadget on his sports watch; he said he was ready for anything. She leaned with both hands on the back of the sofa, her back to the French windows, as a pain wrenched and gathered force.

Calm down. Breathe. She remembered leaning back into Jim's arms on those rubbery hospital mats. She stared at the oatmeal carpet and breathed one, two, three in – pause and then out, one, two, three, four, five. The pain actually melted a little. Again, she pulled the healing oxygen into her lungs. *I can do this; I can.*

The doorbell rang. She dragged herself into the hall. But the shape through the door glass was not Jim's. She slowed down and put the chain on. The door opened just an inch to reveal a slice of Uncle John.

'It's only me. I came to check that you're all right.'

'I – what? I'm fine...'

'Jim asked me to come, to have a chat with you.'

'But he... I'm sorry, it's not a good time.'

'I'll just come in and explain and then I'll let you go. It's really nothing to worry about. Sarah?' She could only see one of his eyes. The white looked raw and exposed.

'Sorry, I can't right now. Jim's on his way.'

'No, Jim sent me.'

'I don't–' He lifted a foot. She jammed the door shut, gasping. She walked away as fast as she could and didn't look back. She got to the sofa and leaned on it as a new pain washed over her. Was Jim really coming? Breathing; do the breathing. Heave in, one, two three, pause and then out, one, two...

There was a crashing explosion behind her. Glass was flying; a metal garden chair thudded into the sofa back; she whirled to see bits of window frame jutting out in jagged ruin. Uncle John stood there, holding a black bag in front of him like a shield.

Purple blood snaked from his hairline into his eye. He stepped through the smashed French windows. Shards of glass tinkled from his clothes and crunched beneath his feet. A scream ripped from Sarah's throat and she swerved around the sofa and backed away. She bumped into the phone table and fumbled behind her for the phone – but he lunged at her and the table tipped up; the phone and the statue crashed to the floor.

Sarah backed further, towards the hallway – the front door. He stepped to the side and the fallen table blocked her way; he came forwards and she shrank into the kitchen.

He advanced and her back bumped against the kitchen table as her contraction peaked. She reeled to the side but one strong hand grasped her hair; the other dumped the black bag on the table. She was penned between his arms. His pupils were black and huge; his skin purple. Cuts gaped on his face and head. He took a long breath as though inhaling her.

Her spine rattled the table. Everything swam and she squeezed her fists. *Don't faint – you can't!* He took his eyes off her face and looked down at her bump.

The knife block was on the worktop, just out of reach. The purple face drained to a sick yellow-white.

'It's because of you that she had to go.' His voice cracked and his hand slipped from her hair. 'Mary's dead!' he said.

The breath was whacked from her chest, but she hurled herself to the side. She clasped a knife handle and pulled with a ringing swish.

'Get away!' The blade glinted in front of her bump. She would plunge it through flesh, sinew, bone, to keep him off her.

But pain dragged at her core, mounted, hardened. Sound muffled. His stare wavered and blurred. Her upper back hit something. She threw out an arm to grip the table edge.

The knife was knocked from her grasp. It clattered to the floor and span away across the tiles. When her vision cleared, he was delving in his bag. Her pain was on the downhill run. Cold liquid squirted in her face. A needle pointed towards her.

She reeled aside and squirmed round the edge of the table, then backed along its length. He was coming after her. The worktop at the rear of the kitchen hit her back. There was no way out. She would never know her baby. Her chest and her womb were bursting. There was a rushing in her ears.

He lowered the syringe towards her middle.

She bellowed 'No!' and her arms flailed against him. The needle pressed the taut skin of her bump. She swung and punched but it pricked through. There was a dark blur in the air. His eyes flared, astonished. Red spurted from his head as if a ripe fruit had burst. His eyes rolled up and he tipped back slowly through the air. There was a clattering thump.

Behind him was Deb. She was holding the pregnant statue in both hands.

Jim unlocked the front door but it only opened a crack.

'Sarah?' Silence. He hurtled at the door, shoulder first. At the third bump it crashed open and they ran through the hall to the living room. 'Sarah!?' No reply. Why was the table on its side; the phone on the floor?

In the kitchen, an unreal scene: Uncle John lay unconscious. Round his head was a shining halo of blood. Beyond this, Sarah lay. Deb was cradling her head in her lap. But Sarah didn't look like someone having a baby; her jaw hung slack and she was deathly still. Jim fell on his knees beside her and shouted her name.

'He was attacking her,' Deb said. 'She collapsed. I think I've killed him.' Her face was spattered with red, and now it was lit up by a blue light, flashing on and off. Sound rushed in and the room was full of uniforms and ear-splitting radio noise. People were barking out words all around Jim, but nothing made sense.

Jim and David held on tight as the ambulance lurched wildly on the woodland track; the paramedic leaning over Sarah could barely stay upright. David's pupils were black and huge like holes blown in his eyes. He was staring at the squad car bumping along behind them. The police had put Deb in the back of it.

'Come on Sarah, wake up for me now.' The paramedic, a wiry older woman, tapped Sarah's cheek with her palm, then listened with a stethoscope pressed to her belly. 'The heart rate has dipped,' she said. 'It means the baby's in distress. We need to bring her round, so she can push.'

Jim struggled to his feet and gripped the edges of the stretcher. 'Sarah! Come on babe, come on!'

'That's great. A familiar voice often works best,' the paramedic said. She looked over at David, too, but he didn't look as though he could speak at all.

'Sarah, I'm sorry,' Jim said. 'Please wake up. The baby's coming. You've got to push.' The ambulance swayed.

There was a sharp crack and a violent swerve. David crashed into Jim as the whole ambulance tipped slightly to the side and came at a standstill, its wheels spinning with a buzz-saw whine.

'Is she okay?! Is she okay?!' Jim called. There was shouting and radio-distorted voices. David was pushing himself out of the human tangle to stand unsteadily upright.

'There's – no change,' the woman said. 'Are you two all right?'

'Yes, why've we stopped?' The wheel noise came to a sudden halt, exposing Jim's shout.

The doors of the ambulance were pulled open by a male paramedic. 'Tree branch fell on us. We're stuck in the mud. I'll call another unit, but if you gents could get out, we'll try to shift this one.' Behind him, the police car had pulled up and two policemen were getting out. Jim watched David step down on trembling legs.

'I'm not leaving Sarah,' Jim said.

'We'll bring her out too.'

Jim crouched over Sarah on her trolley, which stood on the leaf-strewn path. The female paramedic called her name in a calm, bright voice, but Sarah's white face showed no response. All around them was chaos: men were pushing at the back of the ambulance, but it wouldn't budge. The engine shrieked and mud exploded from beneath the wheels.

A male paramedic stepped back from the ambulance, breathing hard, his green uniform splattered with mud. The policemen backed away too, their shoulders slumping.

'Shit. What am I doing?' It was David's voice – he was staring at Sarah. Jim hadn't heard him speak since they were at Woodlands. Now he turned towards the ambulance like someone throwing off a heavy cloak of numbness, and launched himself at it with a roar.

'All right sir, if you'd just stand back!' a policeman shouted, clapping a hand on David's arm.

'I can't stand back – that's my sister! We've got to get this thing moving!' The policeman caught the paramedic's eye, and hesitated. The other man shrugged and motioned him on.

David pressed his shoulder against the right-hand corner of the ambulance, where it was deepest in the mud, and braced his feet against a rock in the path. Others joined him, and voices yelled instructions. The engine started and David hurled his weight at the vehicle. In the roar of the engine and the shrieking of wheels, they heaved.

The gaps in Sarah's eyelids showed the whites of her eyes.

There was birdsong up here in the treetops, and warm, dappled sunlight. Leaves danced in a gentle breeze, and Sarah's pain had gone. Should the pain have stopped? Wasn't it important somehow? But it was so peaceful here. She could let go of everything. The treetops faded into a soft white light. Round the corner of the white corridor, Mummy came towards her. She held out her hands and smiled. Sarah ran to her and strong arms went round her. Soft hair brushed her cheek in a gentle, heady scent.

'She's going off!' The voice was far away.

Leaves rustled again; birds chirped and far below an engine roared. Louder than anything, a man's voice yelled,

'Sarah! Sarah! Please! Wake up, Sarah, for the baby!'

Jim. Pain wrenched her belly. She fell through the air and landed in a rush of noise on a trolley in the woods.

Her insides were heaving in chaos. Contractions! There were things she had to do. Now a freight train was bearing down inside her. It was nothing like the pains before; her insides were rotating and switching positions, like a transformation in a horror film, skin and muscle pushed beyond endurance. Pain was an unstoppable pressure, building towards a crescendo. Then Sarah knew where it was going and she opened her eyes and saw Jim's face. She cried out to him, but all she heard was a guttural noise:

'Agghrrrbshh!'

'What?' He turned to someone beside him, 'What's she saying?'

The force inside her was at bursting point but still powering downwards. She was an animal with only one impulse.

'I gotta push!'

Jim helped prop Sarah up on her elbows. Her chin was on her chest, her face contorted.

'That's it love, you push!' the paramedic shouted.

The engine noise deepened as the wheels finally gripped and, as Jim looked up, the ambulance lurched forward out of the mud, abruptly free.

A policeman clapped David on the shoulder.

'Well done, mate! I never thought we'd shift it.'

The paramedic puffed, 'Adrenaline. It doesn't know the weight of an ambulance. Or the strength of a man.'

And now David, sweating and gasping, gazed at Sarah as if he'd brought her back to life through his own brute power.

They piled back into the vehicles, Sarah on her trolley, and soon they were speeding through the trees. At long last the dark woods ended and they roared out into light.

CHAPTER THIRTY-NINE

Hilary sat on a sofa in the Woodlands reception area. The place was swarming with uniforms. Even DI Martin, head of her old team, had turned up. She had asked someone for a word with him, but was told he was busy talking to the clinic staff. She looked round for him and the room seemed to waver under the great vaulted ceiling. It must be the shift she'd put in. And the shock.

'So, freelancing now, are we?' DI Martin said, rocking the sofa beside her.

'Can't keep away. Any news on the missing nurse?'

'Nothing yet. The uniforms are searching.'

'Do they know the layout of the place? It's like a rabbit warren. There are bits you could miss…' He gave her a look. He had always been scathing about civilians taking it upon themselves to investigate. But surely she deserved more credit? 'I knew something was off about this place from the start. Nurses had been dismissed for asking too many questions. And the staff nurse who showed me round was incredibly aggressive to this elderly patient…' Something was firing in her tired brain. 'Just because he was asking…' She found she had got to her feet.

'What? Where are you going?'

'Just thought of something.'

She pounded down a corridor towards the West Wing with energy from goodness knows where. The DI was following her, grumbling. It took her several tries to find the right room, but there was the same thin old man, sitting on the edge of his bed looking dazed and startled.

'It's Quentin, isn't it? Remember, I was here last night? You were asking about a nurse – you said she was meant to come back and see you, and she didn't?'

It seemed to take an age for him to process her words and formulate his own. 'Well … yes. She promised to come back. She was always true to her word. Never let you down. I keep telling people. No one listens, you see. Apart from her.'

‘I’m listening, Quentin. Did she say where she was going after she left you?’

He frowned, his mouth hanging open. Hilary remembered what the nurse from CareCorps had said about over-medication, and fought down teeth-grinding frustration.

‘Well, let me think… That was it. She was going to change my bed for me. But there wasn’t any bedding.’

‘Right. That’s great Quentin. I don’t suppose you know where they keep the bedding?’

‘I don’t think they like going down there,’ he said, shaking his head. ‘Perhaps that’s why they don’t bother.’ Hilary nodded encouragement. ‘It’s in the basement.’

They jogged along the basement corridor, banging open every door. One, to Hilary’s surprise, revealed not a cupboard or a room, but a dimly lit corridor leading off this one. There was a faint but repellent smell – urine or vomit? And something coppery, festering. She caught the DI’s eye.

‘What’s that noise?’ she whispered.

‘Just the uniforms blundering about upstairs isn’t it?’

But it was more rhythmical than that, a sharp thudding sound. It drew Hilary towards it, and DI Martin followed.

A woman was slumped forwards in an odd squat chair. The back of her head was a mess of blood and her body was shaken by violent spasms. They rushed to her, one on either side, and lifted her upper body. Her head tipped back, showing a livid purple face with the eyes rolled up in their sockets. Hilary saw now why she was hanging so oddly: straps around her arms and waist attached her to the chair. Her name badge was smeared with dried blood.

‘It’s her,’ she said. ‘The missing nurse.’ And then the DI was on his radio, calling for medical assistance.

‘You stay with her,’ he said. ‘I’m going back up to direct them down here.’

Hilary held Kim Saunders upright with a hand on her shoulder and another cupping her chin; she didn’t want to touch that terrible head injury. The poor woman’s body jerked and went rigid one more time, and then slumped into stillness. The place was eerily silent without the clattering of the chair legs against the floor.

‘Hold on, Kim,’ she said. There was a twitch in one blood-encrusted eyelid. A final spasm, or a flicker of response? ‘There’s help coming, Kim. Hold on.’

CHAPTER FORTY

They had reassured Deb countless times. Sarah recounted her research into other cases, Hilary told her about the defence of reasonable force and David held her when she awoke in the bleak dawn hours, and said, 'It won't happen. I'm telling you. It won't.' But they couldn't take this ordeal from her: having to stand here in the dock on shuddering legs while the judge shuffled papers and waited for quiet. It seemed days ago now that she had dropped Joe off at school; had it really been this morning? His hand tightened in hers when they passed another Reception child screaming and clinging to his mother, but then he gave Deb a quick wet kiss and she watched him walk inside as though excited to start his day. He didn't know she might not be going home to him.

She glimpsed David and Hilary, their faces grim – oh, so they weren't so sure that it would all end well? And there was Carol, her lawyer, who said they had every reason to be hopeful, but she never made promises you could cling to. The court usher behind Deb might soon be leading her down to a cell. Would she cry out like that four-year-old? Would she break down and beg? But the judge had started speaking. She dragged in a breath.

'In common law, you are allowed to use reasonable force to prevent an attack on another person. In addition, the Criminal Law Act of 1967 provides that a person may use such force as is reasonable in the circumstances in the prevention of crime. It is quite clear from what we have heard over the past days that the defendant, Deborah Greaves, acted to prevent an attack by the deceased, John Briers, on her friend, Sarah Mercer and on Mrs Mercer's unborn child, at a time when she was uniquely vulnerable. I therefore recommend that the defendant should be entirely acquitted of the charge of manslaughter. Deborah Greaves, I am sorry that you have been put through the anxiety of a trial. I hope that you can now put this matter behind you and get on with your life. You are free to go.'

There were gasps. Applause flapped around Deb like a sudden flight of birds. People were hugging and clapping one another's backs. But Deb's legs were useless and her insides were turning to liquid.

'I don't feel well!' she whispered, and then the court usher was rushing her down the corridor to the Ladies.

'There you are! We thought we'd lost you,' Hilary said when she came out of the toilet stall at last.

'Everything just went,' Deb said. 'My legs were all wobbly, my bowels sort of lurched...'

'Oh! Too much information. I told you they'd acquit you.'

'But you didn't know for sure. No one did.'

Hilary put her arms around her. 'OK I admit, shit does happen in courtrooms. But it didn't today. It's OK.'

The door opened. 'Am I intruding?' Kim said. Deb gestured for her to come in. As she shut the door, Deb saw a patch of short hair at the back of her head. Kim turned and fixed her with her lop-sided gaze; one eyelid drooping a little, and then came and put her arms round her. 'You can have your life back now. I'm not saying it'll be the same as before, but you can do what the guy in the funny wig said. Make it good.'

'Oh God, don't start me off again.' Deb darted into a cubicle, grabbed a few sheets of toilet paper and went out wiping her nose. 'I don't think you've met Hilary.'

'No but I wanted to. You saved my life.'

Hilary flapped a dismissive hand. 'Oh, no. Deb here's the life saver.'

'No, they told me at the hospital – you found me just in time. I wouldn't have lasted much longer. So thank you.'

'Well, it was your testimony that convinced the judge how dangerous Briers was. I know he's not here to convict, but at least the world knows what he did.'

'How are you, Kim?' Deb asked.

'Not bad for an old wreck. I've just finished months of physio and I'm going back to work soon, part time. See how I get on. And I've lost half the vision in this funny-looking eye but, well, I just turn my head.' She demonstrated with a comical head-turn and Deb heard herself laughing.

'Are we ready to face the world?' Kim was nodding towards the door.

Further along the courtroom corridor a nice-looking man was waiting. Beside him, a tall youth and a strawberry-blonde teenager were lounging on a bench. They stood up quickly as Deb and the others drew near.

'Who's that with your two?' Deb whispered.

'Oh, that's Graham. He's a glutton for punishment. Our second date was in intensive care.'

Shouts were barked out over a clamouring crowd outside. 'The press are waiting,' Hilary said.

'Shock horror acquittal in Dr Sicko case,' said Kim.

Hilary's hand was on Deb's arm. 'Carol will make a statement for you. She just needs to know what you want her to say.'

Deb slowed and hung back, unsure of her balance suddenly as if someone had cut the strings that held her upright. 'What am I meant to say? I thought they were going to lock me up away from my child. Where's David, Hilary? I just want to go home to Joe.'

'You do that then. Go home to Joe.' As Graham and her teenagers came over to join them, Kim's gentle smile erased the unevenness from her face.

'Mummy, inner noods.' Ella squirmed out of the bed, her elbow knocking the soft skin below her mother's eye. The clock radio showed 5.54.

'It's too early for the woods, darling.'

'Inner noods.' Ella stood her ground, sought out one of Sarah's hands beneath the duvet and leaned back, tugging. The woods were lovely under the spell of early morning. But tiredness was a constant twilight; what exhausting sequence of actions would get them there? Nappy change, clothes, find shoes. Leaf shadows dappled the curtains, a blackbird chirruped and Ella began to whine.

'All right! Just let mummy get ready.'

Jim's arms folded around her middle, his breath warming the back of her neck. She pulled herself free.

'Where you going?'

'In the noods with Ella.'

Jersey trousers and a sweatshirt were slung over the back of a chair. She pulled them on, then scooped Ella up, assessing the weight and whiff of her nappy along with the sweet squidge of her flesh.

'You're off your rocker.'

'I know that,' she said.

Jim lay, lulled by the rhythmical murmur from the nursery: Sarah's longer and Ella's shorter phrases folding over one another, punctuated by giggles; exclamations; snatches of song. He could drift off now and slip under again. Ella had come into their bed in the night, squirming and fussing for ages before she settled. He needed more sleep; he always did. But it was no good; his mind had sprung alert. He peered at the clock. How soon could he ring?

The legal complications of John Briers' estate were drawing towards resolution, and a hotel chain was interested in the manor house. Now seemed the time to make an offer on the Gatehouse, staking their claim as sitting tenants. He had found out which estate agent Battersea Dogs Home were dealing with, and had even spoken off the record with one of the charity's lawyers.

'It's actually not unusual,' she had said, 'for bequests to be made almost maliciously, at the expense of relatives. But with this one so huge, and the source so – well, infamous – the PR people want it sold on quickly.'

When he had heard about the will, Jim had seen himself in reception that day in his football gear. How stupid to feel the personal slight, with all Briers' other crimes laid bare. Why even care that he had thought Jim a gold-digger and laughed in his face?

Woodlands Clinic had been closed since the discovery of Mary's body. He shuddered once more at the well-worn memories. Sarah had nearly died – he hadn't listened; he hadn't saved her – but after all the shocks and terror of that day, he had been handed his beautiful baby, bellowing, incredible, alive.

He caught himself picking at wounds, working on yet another apology. 'I know you're sorry,' she always said. 'I don't want you to be sorry. It's just another way of us feeling bad.'

'What do you want?' he had asked her once.

'You and Ella.' Her tired voice. 'This place to renovate. A life.'

Anyone else would have abandoned the wreckage and moved miles away. Mum still kept finding them nice little places near her and Dad. But Sarah didn't want this. He pictured himself telling her that he had fixed things, had a word with the lawyer and the estate agent; that the Gatehouse was going to be hers.

The air in the garden was verdant and fresh, reviving Sarah's sleep-hungry senses. She closed the French windows and in her mind, her uncle exploded though them again. Panic surged against her ribs, but she waited for it to pass, watching Ella's toddling progress down the garden. She refused to see him on the bench as they walked past, covering him over with its newer memories: Jim home early to play with Ella; David bringing Joe round after school; Deb and Hilary chatting at weekends. She opened the garden gate and Ella issued forth on impatient little legs. 'See bunnies?' she asked, excitement swelling her voice to a shout.

'Maybe! If we're quiet...' No doubt every creature in the area was taking cover at their approach. Leaf shadows and sunshine tickled the path and wisps of morning mist still clung to the hollows. They made slow progress, with Ella stooping to examine a jewel of moisture on a leaf and again to poke an abandoned snail shell. Yawning and stretching on one of these stops, Sarah glimpsed the Woodlands tower, reaching over the trees.

A question Joe had asked her replayed in the dappled hush. Ella was pottering onwards, heedless and unafraid. Sunlight flashed off the tower window, and Sarah called out before she could think again, 'Ella! Look.' The little girl trotted over and Sarah perched her on her hip. 'Can you see that tower over there, far away in the woods?' She was fairly sure that the wide-eyed gaze was looking in the right direction. 'Well. When you were a tiny baby in my tummy, a lady lived there...' Ella began to twiddle with the hair over her ear, the way she did when you told her a bedtime story. 'She used to look over at our house and think about me, and about you in my tummy, and – she made a wish that we'd be very happy.' Ella's mouth fell open, dribble pooling over the pink swell of her lip, but the next moment she sucked it in and began to wriggle to get down.

Sarah sighed, plonking her on her feet. Ella picked up a forked twig with a cotton-wool tangle of cobwebs, then walked on, entranced by the ferns tickling her legs. Following her, Sarah was wondering how to sweeten the subject of turning back, when Ella spoke. 'Where is it, lady?'

'What lady? Oh! The lady from the tower?'

Ella nodded. Sarah took her hand. 'I'll tell you on the way back to have breakfast with Daddy.' They were walking in the opposite direction before Ella could object. 'Well, she has gone from the tower, which is good, because it wasn't very nice for her to be stuck there. The tower's empty now. And I don't know where the lady is, but I do know that she loved us, and wanted us to be happy.'

They were quiet on the way home, Ella perhaps starting to get hungry. The rest of the day began to take shape in Sarah's mind. She was going for a coffee with Deb, both leaving the children at home with their Dads so they could have a proper catch-up. Perhaps she would tell Deb about this walk with Ella, and her story of the lady in the tower.

As she lifted the latch of the gate and pulled it open, smoke billowed over the garden and a dark figure loomed in her memory, but she blinked and made it go. Ella was running up a clear, bright path towards the French windows, because everything for her was new and unspoiled; and Sarah could see Jim's face at the kitchen window, chin up, expectant, looking out for their return.

Sophie Kersey

Sophie Kersey worked in publishing for almost thirty years before going freelance to pursue her lifelong writing ambitions. She is now a freelance writer and editor. Her articles have appeared in counselling and parenting magazines and in the US collection *Enduring Love.* She is the author of local history book *The History of Halstead Preparatory School. Unspeakable Things* is her first novel. She lives in Kent with her husband, Jon, and has two grown-up sons.

Look out for news on Sophie's website: sophiekerseyauthor.com
Blog: creakydoorwriter.blogspot.co.uk
Facebook page: Sophie Kersey, Author and Twitter: @SophieKersey

QUESTIONS FOR BOOK GROUPS

1. How do you think pregnancy changes Sarah, even before events take a darker turn? Is her curiosity about her background understandable?
2. How does Jim react to Sarah's quest to find out about her mother? Is there anything in his background that might explain his fears for Sarah?
3. Consider the role of friendship in the story. Why might Sarah and Deb both have a particular need for close friendships? What effect does it have on them both when this is threatened?
4. Do you find David's character frustrating or intriguing? Does the reason for his behaviour become clearer?
5. Joe is Sarah's first experience of loving a child before she has her own. Do you sympathise with her distress when this goes wrong, or do you feel more protective towards Joe and Deb?
6. Do you become suspicious of Jim's role as Sarah begins to suspect her uncle is plotting against her? What in Jim's background and character might make him a suspect?
7. What motivates Kim to go out of her way to help the patient in the tower and others? Is it frustrating or understandable that she isn't able to expose what is going on earlier?
8. What do the woods symbolise in the novel?
9. What role does Kim's faith have in her story? How does she feel about it when things go so horribly wrong for her?
10. Did you believe that Uncle John's revelations from the past were true? Or were you always suspicious of him?
11. Does the twins' childhood explain what John has become? What might have led to his reaction to Sarah's pregnancy?
12. Compare the two weddings in the novel. What connects them?
13. Which characters are the potential rescuers in the novel? Who are you most hopeful will help those in jeopardy?
14. Is Sarah a passive victim? Does she strike you as resilient as the story unfolds? How about at the end?

42127666R00125

Printed in Poland
by Amazon Fulfillment
Poland Sp. z o.o., Wrocław